The VOICES of the DEAD

Dark **Tales** & **Lost** Souls
An **Anthology** of the **Endlands**

by
Scott Fitzgerald Gray

Cover, Design, and Typography
by **(studio)Effigy**

Published by **Insane Angel Studios**
insaneangel.com

Monumental
WORKS GROUP

The VOICES of the DEAD

Dark **Tales** & **Lost** Souls
An **Anthology** of the **Endlands**

For **Harlan Ellison**

Don't be afraid.
That simple; don't let them scare you.

Be silent in that solitude
Which is not loneliness, for then
The spirits of the dead who stood
In life before thee are again
In death around thee, and their will
Shall overshadow thee: be still.

— Edgar Allan Poe,
"Spirits of the Dead"

— The **Moonsign** Scar —

"DO YOU LOVE ME?" she whispered like she had whispered so many times before, and the low rasp of his breathing as he clung trembling to her gave her the answer better than any words.

Shadow and faint firelight cloaked Sharyna where she moved in gentle rhythm, far from the light of evenlamps washing the walls with cold flame. Closer to the bed and its twisted field of furs, three braziers smoldered low, all of them burning bright when the night had begun. The chamber was round like the tower it stood within, black like the stone of the outside walls and the heart of the bearded figure who lay helpless as a child beneath her, staring up at her pale face within its shroud of black hair.

Skos Andarost was the name the mage had been born with, but it had been a generation since he had been known as anything other than Jarrn Dark Andarost. The tattoos that snaked across his arms and chest marked him as one of the Jarrnath, the sorcerous order that had long since spread from its birthplace in Ajaeltha, north to the Gracian wilderness and the Vanyr frontier where the ever-present threat of war masked the movements and madness of its members. The legendary depravity of his kind should have frightened Sharyna. The whispered rumors of Andarost's individual deeds should have frightened her even more.

When she was eleven, she'd been made to watch her parents die. Tortured first, then sacrificed on the living pyres of the Cynuss cultists of the Vanyr. Even by the standards of war, those four years of bloodshed across the frontier had been particularly brutal.

It had been a long time since Sharyna was afraid.

Two months past, she had stepped through the arches of the front gates under escort of the house-slave who had purchased her. The perfect note of longing in the sorcerer's voice as she moved slowly astride him now was the perfect culmination of everything she had worked for in that time. Growing close to him, following the line of timid devotion that the guise she wore demanded. Allowing his initial depravations in the name of the eventual dependency that had slowly turned him, slowly twisted him between the fingers she raked across his chest now.

Then he was up against her, deep inside her, clutching her tight, and the last thing Andarost saw was her smile.

She had three vials in her mouth, carefully glued to the inside of her teeth months before. Hollow slivers of translucent ilvanglass, two holding six measured drops each of tasteless liquids whose power was unleashed only when mixed. She felt the glass cut her, tasted the salt tang of blood as she shattered the vials with two swift movements of her tongue.

She could have killed him. That was how closely she had worked herself into Andarost's life in only two months. But the carefully measured dosage she let fall to his open mouth where it found hers would let him wake once her work was done. More importantly, it would make him understand.

For all of them, for every man or woman who had ever felt that kiss, it was first and foremost about leaving them to understand.

The third vial held the antitoxin, but she cracked it for only herself as Andarost collapsed to the bed. And when the unnatural slumber had taken him, she found the hidden latch of the chamber's unseen door and stepped naked into the chill of the corridor beyond.

The drug was a pankova variant for which the Sisters of Sorrow alone knew the recipe. Like pankova in all its raw forms, it had both narcotic and cognitive effect. The variant that Sharyna had fed to Andarost — that she fed to every target the sisterhood had directed her to seek and destroy — amplified both effects with a precision that had taken three generations of alchemists to achieve.

Through the night, Andarost would sleep. But when he awoke, he would understand with that unnatural pankova clarity how completely he had offered his heart to Sharyna and the promise of love she made to him. How completely and irrevocably she had used that offer to break him.

The main hall beyond the chamber was as empty as the rest of the tower. Andarost's contempt for those he considered beneath him inspired a solitude that made Sharyna's work that much easier. But as she padded silently along the carpeted gallery, she heard the faintly thudding movements of Liask on the bare stones of an adjacent alcove. She glanced back to see the raven hopping toward her with its familiar awkward gait.

She ignored the bird with practiced ease, even as she fought the unsettling feeling that it had always taken some sort of perverse pleasure in her nakedness. She felt a chill across breast and back, at the still-wet smoothness of her sex as she summoned up the trigger force for the incantation of returning from within herself. Through a veil of white light that materialized from empty air, she pulled clothing and cloak, dagger and side sword, ring and pendant from out of their hiding place in an outskirts village at the mountain's foot. She had scouted there six months before, paying a farmer for a year's root-cellar storage of a footlocker that would prove empty when he realized she wasn't returning for it.

All around her, Sharyna felt the faint tingling of Andarost's sorcerous wards as they went off at the casting of her own spell — his defenses active and worthless where he lay comatose in the bedchamber behind her. She dressed quickly, slipped the ring on to feel its protective force trace out to wrap her body like a subtle shell. Around her neck, she pulled the pendant on its leather thong. An amethyst teardrop alchemically inlaid with lines of gleaming silver. An image was rendered there, three nails intercrossed above an open palm, fingers spread. The symbol of the sisterhood, well worn where Sharyna's hands had clutched it tight each night those first months after her parents died.

She slung the weapons on last. The sword was a field blade whose length and weight were an incongruous match for her lissom frame, her gracefully muscled arms. The dagger was a bone-handled blade of the Norgyr, and like the sword, she had been taught to use it by a warrior she knew, long ago now. He had fallen in love with her, like all the rest. What she had felt for him in return wasn't something she let herself give a name to now.

She lost sight of the bird as she made her way quickly down the stairs. She felt its black gaze following her, though. A familiar sensation since the day she arrived. Andarost's inner chamber where she and the mage had lain together was virtually the only place in the tower off limits to that gaze, but she had seen Liask more often than she liked lingering atop the bookcases outside the hidden doors. Almost as if the creature recognized the hold she was slowly developing over its master. Resenting her. If so, the feeling was mutual.

It had been a half-day's walk up the mountainside track under escort. A unique opportunity, the house-slave had told Sharyna as she knew he would. His master a powerful and influential figure, with a place for one such as her in his household. She had gone meekly, knowing what the offer meant in a way that none of the others who had walked that twisting track before her had known. Knowing that from the moment Andarost set eyes on her, the bargain would be changed.

As she descended past narrow windows, she saw the city lights below, the sorcerer's tower rising from the mountain cleft above it like a black spike. Impressive enough from a distance. But up close, one could see where its stones had crumbled, rough mortar patches hastily slapped on and darkened with ash. Pretense patchwork hiding the weakness of a crumbling strength, not unlike Andarost's grim demeanor had hidden the fatal longing that had granted Sharyna entrance to this tower, to his life.

At the foot of the stairs, three corridors opened up. The main doors of the tower gate lay straight ahead down a wide space of black stone and statuary, but she wasn't bound there. Not yet.

Far down the west corridor lay the servants' wing, light spilling from beneath the door of the kitchens as Sharyna paced silently toward it. She laid a hand on the hilt of the sword as she pushed her way through.

A score of faces close to a central blazing firepit turned to stare as one. A dozen men and women, the Humans and Half-Ilvani of the northlands. Nearly as many children between them, the youngest barely walking. Beyond them, crates and barrels clustered in shadow along the walls. Woodsmoke and the scent of roast meat twisted through the torchlight, hung heavy in the air. Sharyna's gaze flicked across it all, but settled on the scarred wooden table in the farthest corner of the oversized chamber. There, the house-slave sat.

Sanos he called himself, perched in his chair, feet up as he drained the last dregs of a tankard and traded it for another already set up before him. Hair grey, face lined with contempt more than age. Back straight but shoulders stooped above thick arms. He watched her with a wary detachment that almost hid his surprise.

"Heed my words," Sharyna called. "Andarost the master of this place has engaged in foulness beyond any indignities he metes out on you who serve him. For that, he has been called to account and found wanting. Leave now. Take your lives, take your freedom and go. You have till dawn."

There was the moment of stunned silence she had expected as she paced the room.

"He will kill you," she said simply. "He will seek revenge on whoever is closest to him when he cannot find me. Save yourselves and your children."

"And what exactly is it you've done, whipling?" It was Sanos. He leaned his chair back against the wall, drank deeply.

"Hurt him," Sharyna said where she circled closer. The house-slave laughed.

"The fact you're standing here and not spread as ash down the stairs tells me you got the drop on him somehow, which I'll give full credit for. But Dark Andarost don't get hurt by the likes of you."

She stopped in front of him, raised her leg to punch his chair down with a carefully placed foot between his thighs. Whatever he was drinking sloshed across him. The house-slave's gaze was dark but he stayed where he was, Sharyna's eyes locked to his.

"For Andarost to follow you to the city would be to admit publicly that he has been bested by me," she said to the room, but there was an edge in her voice now. "Get yourselves there, you will be safe. Seek better lives beyond if you can. Go."

As one, the assembled servants scattered for the dark hanging blankets that marked the sleeping area off the fire. Sanos ignored them, watching Sharyna as he drained his second mug. When he was done, he crushed it slowly in both hands. The groan of spun pewter was loud in the silence.

"I take my freedom, whipling," he said quietly. "None gives it to me, least of all cult-fodder like you."

As his dark gaze flicked down, Sharyna felt it seek out the amethyst hanging at her neck. She remembered that gaze appraising her the night he brought her to the tower, a whispered incantation forcing his eyes to hers over all the other girls cowering in the brothel common room.

With a fluid motion, she had sword and dagger drawn and held steady a single stride from Sanos where he sat. Body ready and locked for a thrust he had no space to avoid, but far enough away that though he might block one blade, he wouldn't stop both. The warrior had taught her that.

"I give the others their freedom, house-slave. You're with me."

Up the inner staircase that wound above the open court below, Sanos climbed ahead of her at swordpoint, Sharyna wary. She marked him as ex-military by his demeanor, and a criminal according to the brand at his neck — the triple-stroked rune of treason and the Gracian griffon burned into his flesh as permanent record of offense against the state. Whether Andarost had bought him legally or Sanos had fled to servitude after escaping the labor camps, she couldn't guess. The scar tissue of the brand was ageless pink, but the skin around it had been darkened by long years that said it didn't matter anymore.

"Know where you're going, do you?" As he called, Sanos didn't look back.

"Andarost's laboratory," she said. "You've never been there." Not a question.

"Not my place to be there."

"But you've collected his specimens for half a year. Bought them on his behalf. You'll bury them when he's done."

"I do my job," the house-slave murmured.

Sharyna could feel the effort of the climb in her legs already, the staircase circling around the tower for the second time now. Ahead of her, Sanos wasn't even breathing hard.

"Your job," she echoed. "Collecting sentient beings to be used as fodder for a madman's craft."

"You ever actually spent time in a Makas brothel?" he said easily. "Aside from the one night you waited there for me and used whatever charm it took to get me leading you back here?" Sharyna hadn't told him, but the house-slave had already deduced his unwitting part in her game. "You ever see a child addicted to eus by a whoremonger's hand? Tortured for nobles' sport? You come down from your masochist's cloister, sister, you'd know there's things worse than death."

Ahead, the evenlamps spilled into sudden shadow, the stairs ending where a narrow corridor angled to the right, into the center of the tower. Sharyna stopped to stare at the dark stone door at the corridor's end as if she was checking for threats. In truth, she needed a moment to catch her breath.

"Andarost's ambitions are fueled on things worse than death," she said. "Pain is a gift whose purpose is to remind us we live. Those who inflict suffering too often set themselves above it. They must be reminded otherwise."

Sanos spat. "Save the cult-sermon for someone else," he said. "Why are we here?"

Sharyna stepped past him. She touched the door with the ring key she had liberated from Andarost's hand.

Almost a year past, she'd heard the story from a midwife and healer who worked the brothels in Makas. Dark tales of women, girls, boys disappearing from their servitude in the city. Purchased by a buyer who hid the same treason-brand Sanos wore. Escorted out by him, taken up into the shadow of the mountain, and never seen again.

When her parents died, Sharyna's life had been spared for the contribution she would make to the ranks of the Cynuss cult's breeding program. But when a guard came to the initiate cells one cold night to welcome her to her new place in the world, she punched one still-small hand in through his eye-socket and watched him fall, screaming.

He had been fourteen at best. A farmhand by the set of his shoulders before the cult claimed him. The fear in his face as she strangled him with her own chains was something Sharyna had never forgotten.

As the door swung wide, she heard Sanos choke. A sound of stark disbelief, of fear from one who might well have thought there was nothing that could frighten him anymore.

The chamber was white and black, dark pillars rising between smoothly plastered fascia, a dozen strides along each side. Reflected in a floor of delicate marble, evenlamps hung above a scattered expanse of tables and shelves, pestles and scroll cases, bottles and phials in ordered wooden racks.

On the other three walls, crosses of black iron hung side by side, perhaps thirty in all. In the captives that hung from those crosses, she could see sudden movement, a frantic ripple of fear spreading from the open door.

From along the wall came the faint trickle of a run-off trench. Closest to her, she could see a Human girl, fifteen perhaps. She thrashed mutely, gagged and bound, manacle-clamps holding her at the wrists and ankles. She wore the same shapeless shift they all wore, caked with the filth that clung to her, though the air was clear somehow. Some lingering incantation scrubbed away the reek that should have accompanied such a place, leaving a pleasant air that twisted Sharyna's stomach more than any stench.

The girl recognized Sanos. Sharyna saw the fear in her eyes.

"Blood and moon forgive me," the house-slave whispered.

With all her strength, Sharyna caught him across the back with the flat of the sword, though she knew he would barely feel it. He stumbled ahead, turned on her with fury in his eyes, but she kept her dagger level on his heart.

"Blood and moon might forgive, but I don't," she said. "Free them. Those who can walk, you'll help to carry those who can't. Get them clothes from the servants' quarters, then lead them to the city and to safety. Abandon them and there's nowhere you can hide that I won't find you."

The last was a lie, but Sanos only nodded. Together, they worked their way around the room from opposite sides, releasing Andarost's terrified captives one by one. Sharyna summoned the life-magic for those who needed it, focusing the power of her animys to heal them as best she could. Mending their bodies, at least, but the healer's arts were the least part of the spellcraft she had trained to. No way for her to know if they had the strength in them to ever heal the subtler scars of what had gone on between those white walls.

The one she couldn't save, she killed. A once-graceful Ilvani who had bitten off his own tongue, and who thrashed now in the throes of a silent scream. He was cruciform like all the rest, but as he convulsed, Sharyna saw ribs and spine, bone and joint twisting beneath his skin as if they had life of their own. Some arcane mutilation whose power she could sense as her spell of healing broke uselessly against it.

With an incantation, she made him sleep. He collapsed against her as she loosed him from his black iron cross, laid him gently to the floor. While he slept, she summoned up the healing magic again, felt the familiar pulse of blood and life that drove the animyst power within her. Then she twisted it in the careful way that would drain the life force instead of augmenting it.

With a touch, she felt the frail shell of the Ilvani's life collapse. In the set of his bloodstained lips, she thought she saw peace as he slipped away.

On the Ilvani and one other of Andarost's victims, a Human girl already dead when Sanos brought her down, Sharyna saw the mark.

Along the upper arm, nearly at the shoulder, faint impressions of blood-stippled skin. Two crescents interlocking, offset at right angles, a uniform bruising like something had been struck there.

"They're ready."

Sanos called from the doorway, Andarost's prisoners behind him. More fear than hope in their eyes, Sharyna saw. In his arms, the house-slave held a diminutive Ryta whose right leg was lamed and beyond Sharyna's ability to mend. One of the plains-dark small folk, the traders who descended on the city each spring. She was trembling, Sanos clutching her like a child.

"Lead them down," she said. "I'll catch you up."

"What have you got to wait for?" he said gruffly.

"Go."

She watched him turn for the corridor and the stairs, the others following without a word. As their shuffling footsteps faded, Sharyna paced through the torture chamber, tried to find the distance that she would need to report to the sisterhood what she had found there. But even with all she had seen in the long years of doing sorrow's work, all her young life before then spent learning the ways of the order and the rigid code that bound it, something was different this time.

She had seen slavery. She had been enslaved herself more than once, and had endured all that entails. She had seen petty sadism and political brutality and cult-driven mass slaughter. She had seen all the shades of power and the corruption it bred, and she had brought down its self-styled monarchs by the same subtle manipulation that had felled Andarost this night. But in this place, there was a darkness she could sense but not name. Some vague unease that had been with her since she entered the sorcerer's company.

She passed the crosses one by one, close enough to feel the dark power in them. And though she had time to investigate fully, she had no stomach for it in the end. The unnaturalness of the place tore at her. The sweet air, the walls and floor gleaming in the glow of magical light like some obscene throne room.

From within the secret pocket inside her sleeve, she pulled a packet wrapped in foiled lead. She unwrapped it carefully, revealed a small square of jade graven with a faint glyph. Sharyna had carried the rune-stone since her first mission on the sisterhood's behalf, all the order's agents holding a reserve of power beyond their own that they hoped would never have to be used. But though she knew she should have saved the stone's spell, Sharyna felt an instinct take her that she only partly understood. She felt the power of her blood pulse in her hand, triggering the greater power of the stone as the glyph flared with white light. And then she was stumbling back to the corridor as the laboratory and the darkness she felt there was torn apart by a storm of living fire.

She felt the heat, heard the crack of stone and plaster and the groan of twisting steel. But even harsher, she felt a fear rooting in her that she couldn't explain, felt the pulse of magical power around her as she whispered an incantation of detection. The difference between the arcane force and the animys of life-magic normally presented itself as clear as night and day, but she felt something different here. A dark commingling, a confusion in the power that pulsed and shredded before her as she watched the crosses melt to slag through a haze of white flame.

Behind her, she heard the raven Liask's hoarse croak. A faint echo above the fire's roar that saved her life.

As she glanced back, Sharyna saw the naked Andarost stagger up the stairs at the corridor's end. Instinctively, she summoned the life-energy that was her spellpower, expelling it as a molten bolt. The incantation Andarost had been whispering died on his lips as he screamed.

The sorcerer stumbled back toward the stairs, managed to right himself. Black welts smoldered across his tattooed chest and shoulder, Sharyna seeing the rage in his eyes as he shrugged off the pain.

"You'll need to do a great deal better than that," Andarost whispered, but Sharyna said nothing. Just stared to where the sorcerer clutched her pendant in his shaking hand. She didn't have to reach for her neck to feel it gone, fallen at some point on the climb, she guessed. The leather thong somehow unwound, swinging gently now from the mage's gnarled fingers.

"Sister of Sorrow," Andarost said thickly, "I know your whore's game. Your every thought, your every move in this charade are clear to me now." The sorcerer's words were slurred, his movements erratic. His body was slick with sweat, muscles ridged and twisted with a wholly unwilling tension. The residual effects of the drug that Sharyna recognized, but how could he have overcome it so quickly? Her thoughts were racing, scanning the shadows for a means of escape, but behind her where the laboratory consumed itself and ahead where Dark Andarost raised his hands were her only choices.

"You embrace pain?" the sorcerer hissed. "Then embrace me..."

Sharyna moved, nowhere to go but forward even as she felt the pulse of Andarost's arcane power. A dozen strides to reach him, but she would be dead before she got there.

Liask saved her for the second time then.

From the darkness of the open stairs, the raven erupted like a bolt of living shadow, striking silently to rake its talons across Andarost's face. It gave her the moment she needed, spellpower seething in her as she sprinted past and touched the sorcerer. She saw his eyes consumed by shadow that he clutched at, too late. As she snatched the pendant from his hand, she ducked past, left him staggering, blinded as she flipped over the balustrade and hit the stairs at a run.

All the long way down, she half-expected death to take her at the next step. But whether Andarost had no magic to counter the life-curse she had laid on him or was simply too enraged to use it, she didn't know. She was past the now-deserted servants' quarters when she realized she'd lost sight of the raven as well, but the lingering question of what had prompted the creature's coming to her aid was lost beneath the question of how Andarost had awoken in the first place. The dosage had been perfect, no mistake made. Some magical ward she hadn't sensed, perhaps. A permanent antitoxin in his system, undiscovered despite long days of careful preparation.

Sharyna had been found out before. More than once, she'd been forced to flee from an intended victim, and she knew what her fate would have been those times if she had failed. But her manipulation of emotion, the hold she created on those she destroyed, usually worked in her favor — keeping them from unleashing their full strength against her by virtue of the longing that still lingered in them.

The effects of the drug were different in Andarost, though. A lifetime's pent-up longing brought to the surface in the past two months. The emptiness that came with a certain type of power and the fear of weakness that drove men like him inside themselves. All of it turned to rage now.

She had done what she meant to do. She had been even more successful in it than she'd hoped. Now she had to live long enough for it to make a difference.

She was taking the last stairs to the main hall two at a time when she felt again the surge of arcane power around her. With a crack like shattering wood, Andarost appeared from empty air three strides away, but Sharyna was ready, drawing sword and dagger as she spun and let the force of her movement slash twice into the sorcerer's side. Then she was past him again and racing for the doors, fighting for breath as she ran.

Ahead, she saw Sanos staring back at her.

He had the Ryta still in his arms, was shepherding the last three of Andarost's victims toward the open doors. The others were already outside, dressed in the clothing the servants had left behind, visible in the evenlamp glow that lit the narrow stone bridge at the mouth of the mountain track.

As Andarost stumbled down the stairs, his gaze flicked from Sharyna to the house-slave, cold. She heard the snarled incantation but was already whispering the life-magic's own song.

Even as the sorcerer raised his hands, Sharyna summoned up fire again, drove a blood-red blast into him with all the power she could muster. She saw his eyes seek her as he cried out, his attention pulled from Sanos for the moment the house-slave would need.

A taloned claw of blue-white lightning drove Sharyna back to the far wall, and she swallowed the scream she wanted to make as its searing heat twisted through her. She felt the ring take the brunt of the damage, knew that she wouldn't have survived without it. Even so, her cloak and tunic shredded as she rolled, the arcane claw slamming on past her to strike the doors in an arc of blue-white light.

Through the haze, Sharyna thought she might have seen Sanos glance back. Then he was gone where the wall of the archway had collapsed. The Ajaelthan tapestries and rugs of the hall were burning around her as she scrambled to her feet, a whirlwind of ash and flame eclipsing the dark figure that strode toward her.

Even as she tried to get her bearings, Sharyna felt a fierce tug at her hair. Liask pulled at her with hooked talons, but even as she instinctively batted the raven away, it broke off, winging its way along a narrow side corridor that she might have missed in the haze.

She waited for Andarost to come to her, hoping that his desire to watch her die slowly was strong enough to draw him in. She feigned injury, dragging the sword feebly as she stumbled away, dagger out of sight, focusing on his footsteps.

She whirled, arcing the sword out again. But even as Andarost dodged clear of the intended distraction, she grazed him with her dagger hand. She felt the pulse of power surge through her touch as Andarost screamed, his body wracked with the crippling convulsions she forced upon him. Then she had sword and dagger sheathed and was racing along the narrow corridor, the raven visible in the distance where it circled back, waiting for her. No idea what the creature's game was. No other options than to trust it now.

When she was eleven, her would-be attacker's keys had opened her cell and the others alongside it. How many others fled with her, she didn't know, nor how many of those might have survived the frost of the early winter or the wolves that prowled the frontier steppes. But as she raced for the darkness beyond the torchlit perimeter of the Vanyr village, Sharyna had felt a hand in hers, heard a voice in her ear telling her she had the strength to rise above the ache of cold and the long night's run.

Her name was Acondra, a few years older than Sharyna. She had shown her how to hold on.

Sharyna had only passed once through the maze of corridors on the lower floor during her preliminary explorations of Andarost's tower. The storerooms to both sides stood mostly empty now, reminders of when the citadel must have played home to more than just Andarost and his mad ambition. Then after a half-dozen turns down seemingly identical passages, Liask suddenly dropped, hopping toward the wall. In the intermittent glow of evenlamps, Sharyna saw the bird look back to her, felt the unnatural intelligence in its dark gaze. It took hopping flight again, slamming its wings repeatedly against dark stone.

As she stepped close, Sharyna felt the wall calling.

It was a subtle sensation, something between touch and sound. A kind of pressure pulling at her. And as she laid her hand against it, she felt the power within the wall seeking her in a way she didn't understand. Some kind of conduit for the life-magic she wielded that made no sense in a sorcerer's lair.

At her feet, Liask hissed, an unsettling sound. In the distance, Sharyna heard Andarost's screaming fade to silence. As the magic of animys spun within her, she stripped out one of its twisting threads, focused it as she did when fueling the spells locked tight in her heart and memory. As the magic pulsed within her, she felt the stones of the wall pull it from her, drink her power greedily.

With a weary grinding, the section of wall she touched was pulled slowly in. Sharyna slipped back, wary as she plucked an evenlamp from the opposite wall. Liask hopped ahead, screeching in what she understood was a plea for her to follow.

Betrayal...

Down the maze of corridors behind her, Sharyna heard Andarost's muffled shout. Ahead, a narrow hallway plunged straight on into shadow, no place to be trapped with a vengeful sorcerer behind you.

Sharyna strained to push against the stones of the wall where they had shifted, managed to drive them back almost into position. However, if there was a way to seal them again, it was beyond her understanding, a faint crack of light still showing despite her best efforts to close it. She sent out a tentative tendril of animys again, but whatever force had sought her power out a moment before was gone now.

Betrayal...

"Move," she hissed to the raven. Whether it understood or not, Liask hopped into step behind her as she slipped into the darkness.

She counted sixty steps before that dark was split with a sudden flare of blue-white. A spike of fear kept both hands at her blades as she tried to check her frantic breathing.

Deep within the foundations of the tower, a chamber of white stone opened up. Circular, twenty paces or more across, it rose to a three-arched dome whose light came from no source she could see. Along the walls, cushioned stone benches sat at intervals. Shelves piled with scrolls and bound folios rose high, set in inverse steps along the inward-leaning walls.

She heard the flap of wings as Liask took to the air and soared past her, shrieking an unearthly echo that almost eclipsed Andarost's still-distant scream.

Betrayal...

In the center of the chamber, a pillar of silver-grey crystal rose, five paces in diameter where the light played across it in gently pulsing waves. Around it, the raven soared, black wings beating loud in the silence.

On the pillar's surface, engraved in white lines so bright that they hurt to look at, Sharyna saw a symbol she recognized. The two narrow crescents, cutting through each other like she had seen marked in blood beneath the skin of Andarost's victims she was too late to save.

The moonsign was the symbol of magic across the Elder Kingdoms and through the wide world beyond. The bright Clearmoon given reverence for the life-magic pulse of animys power, circling fast every twenty-nine nights. The red Darkmoon as the symbol of the lingering power of the arcane force, advancing more slowly across the sky. The moonsign of Isheridar was rendered as image in countless ways, and though this specific interlocking of crescents was something that Sharyna would swear she had never seen before, it was hauntingly familiar to her just the same.

Why it was here, what it meant, she didn't know. She heard it calling to her, though. Like the door that had led her here, the symbol on its pillar wordlessly touched the places inside Sharyna where her magic lived.

Sharyna reached for the pillar, touched warm stone. Around her, the raven circled, still shrieking, desperate in a way she could feel. Like an offering, Sharyna gave of the power within her. She felt a kind of cold hunger draw the life-magic from her again.

"Betrayal..."

Behind her, Andarost. Not with the sudden slam of a spatial jaunt, but stepping out from a haze of vapors that had materialized in the wall, a spell Sharyna didn't recognize.

Even as she wheeled, she saw the pillar suddenly split in four and push outward as it drank her power. Opening just as the wall had opened, it revealed a hollow space within where a pedestal of black iron rose. Sitting atop it, a thin steel chain was looped around an amulet of black stone the size of her hand.

The stone was the source of the hunger she felt, stronger now. Etched across its smooth surface in fine lines, she saw the moonsign again.

Sharyna launched another crimson bolt of living fire, but Andarost was ready this time, dismissed it with a wave of his hand. Beneath her, she felt gravity suddenly twist as she was smashed back against the floor. Then she was lifted, suspended motionless in mid-air as the sorcerer stepped slowly toward her and she thought of the laboratory. Pinned helpless like all the rest, like the Ilvani consumed by the twisted mix of magical forces she had felt in the black iron crosses.

But as Andarost stopped in front of her, she saw something in his eyes that chilled her far more than the sadistic darkness. More than the blood-rage that had been there before.

The sorcerer was afraid.

"So this is your game revealed at last, acolyte. I see it all now. Thank you for that…" Andarost's eyes were narrow slits, unfocused. Sharyna tried desperately to think.

She heard the sudden flutter of black wings. She saw Andarost's gaze shift past her, the fear in his eyes burning brighter.

She understood then. She had one chance.

She felt the spell release her as Andarost stumbled back, and following an instinct she only barely understood, Sharyna leapt for the pillar, through the closest opening to snatch at the chain even as she drew the bone-handled dagger.

Behind her, she felt the surge of power that was Andarost unleashing everything left within him in a single blast of arcane fury, white-hot as it boiled from his hands. But he had turned away from her, and as she scrambled back, Sharyna saw that Liask was the mage's target, the raven consumed by molten spellfire.

She forced herself to look away as she dropped to the floor, spinning the dagger to slash a rough circle around her across cold stone. She spoke her spell with a shout, triggering the protective aura that surged and spread from the unbroken line of that faint scratch.

Before her, she saw Andarost's arcane power turned against him, shrouding him like a rain of dark fire. She saw the sorcerer struck down, had to avert her eyes as his limbs and neck were shattered, his entrails unfurling through a haze of blood where his sex and belly were torn open as by unseen knives. And in spite of all she knew of the sorcerer's madness, in spite of all she had seen and burned away in his laboratory, his scream tore at her like a broken blade thrust deep in her gut as the fire turned blue to black and Andarost was consumed.

The fear held in the dark mage's eyes at the last was burned into her memory. Sharyna tried to focus as she slowly turned to the creature that had killed him.

Dark flame writhed around the beast that had been Liask, leering as it advanced slowly toward her. It stood as tall as two men though it walked low on six stunted limbs, its tail lashing the marble of the floor with a sundering crack at each step. Clawed wings swept back from its forelimbs, their translucent skin set with veins that coursed blue-black fire. Its gnarled sex jutted out beneath a rippling belly, spewing fire like a spitting serpent. From the beast's maw, a triple-forked tongue of red-black flicked through a maze of soot-smeared teeth, edged like razored knives. Its long, narrow head bore a sweeping set of jagged horns above the ridges of its burning eyes.

Liask's eyes, Sharyna saw. Still the same dark cunning there. No telling how long the creature had taken the form of the sorcerer's familiar, but she already understood why.

In her hand, the amulet she had been led to was pulsing in perfect rhythm with the pounding of her heart.

Seven passings of the pale moon...

In Sharyna's mind, the creature's voice was the taste of bile. A wave of sudden nausea twisted through her.

Seven months within the mockery-shell of this sun-slaked sphere and the constant torment of its abominations. Seven months to slip inside the mage's life, take his trust, set the tendrils of control in his mind without notice. Control ruined by thee, Sister of Sorrow.

"My thoughts are my own," Sharyna hissed, trying hard to bury the fear. "Stay out of my head."

The beast laughed then, fire flaring where its tongue flicked toward her. With as much bravado as she could feign, Sharyna held her dagger before her, clutched the glowing amulet tight to her breast.

She saw the dark eyes flicker.

Set aside the stone and thou mayest die quickly... the creature whispered.

"Take it if you can..."

The beast reared up to full height, tail and bone-taloned foreclaws slashing deep gouges from the floor. All around her, Sharyna felt the black flame lash out, its heat like the heart of a forge. She felt the creature's scream of rage twist through her.

She had guessed right, though. Like her, the creature had come to Andarost's on a mission of deception, but even brought this close to its goal with her unwitting aid, it couldn't breach the life-magic that protected the black stone it sought. Her power surged in the current of animys coursing through the warding circle she had made. The same animyst power that fueled the wards of the crystal pillar that kept the creature at bay.

She was a perfect proxy, she thought. The beast had awoken Andarost. It had stolen her pendant with sorcery of its own to lead the mage on, then had led Sharyna to this place in her desperation to escape. Her life-magic was the key, somehow.

Indeed, the creature hissed in response, her thoughts still open to it. *Now, Sister of Sorrow, I complete my mission...*

From within the circle's dying defenses, Sharyna summoned the very last of the animyst power that lived in her, raised a barrier forged of her own will and strength, and of the power that sorrow showed her when will and strength were gone. Tendrils of light lashed out from her hand, twisting as they struck. But even as the creature recoiled, Sharyna knew it wasn't enough.

Another wave of unearthly heat hit her as the blue fire pressed in again. She felt the strength of the protective circle begin to crack beneath the beast's assault. She felt the remnants of her cloak and tunic burned away, her belt and scabbards smoldering as shadow and flame wreathing her nakedness. The ring burned at her finger as it drank the power that pushed beyond the circle, its ability to protect her almost gone. She was on the ground, the pain beyond anything she had ever felt. But with the strength born of a short lifetime dedicated to that pain, she moved past it. Felt the clarity that would let her die with a peace her parents had never known.

She felt the black amulet's hunger then.

Between her clutching fingers, Sharyna saw the twin moonsign etched upon the black stone flare, her pain threading through her like forge-hot wire. Blue-black light flared from the corner of her eye, and at her shoulder, she saw the moonsign scar. The same mark that the dead in Andarost's laboratory had borne, the pattern smoldering on her skin. Her pulse was hammering, the mark flaring in time with her pain. Feeding on it.

Sharyna felt a sudden clarity that focused and shaped itself through the agony that pressed in from all sides. She saw the flame blaze hotter in the beast's hands, tendrils lancing off to strike her like a swarm of burning insects. She felt the circle shudder for the last time, felt the creature's triumph as it leered, filling her with a laughter that cut like glass knives.

You embrace pain? An echo of Andarost's words, the creature in the sorcerer's mind like it had been in hers the whole time. *Embrace me...*

Sorrow was the currency of life itself, Acondra had told Sharyna her first night under the sisterhood's protection. They had walked four days to a town whose name she never learned, found a safehouse there in the network of such places the order ran along the borderlands.

Pain is strength, Sharyna had been taught. *Pain is the mirror-image reflection of life. The contrast and shaper of life, as the darkness shapes our understanding of the light.*

As the amulet fed on her, she understood suddenly. The pain that had slowly crippled and killed Andarost's victims had been channeled to the black stone just as her own pain was channeled to it now. The drained space of the animys within her was suddenly filled, the stone somehow turning pain into the potential for the life-magic. Amplifying animys a hundredfold, a thousandfold as Sharyna fought to keep it from overwhelming her.

The agony should have crippled her, the amulet claiming her life as it fed on her pain. But what neither Andarost nor the creature as it raged could possibly have understood was that Sharyna had mastered her pain, long ago now.

From the space of her suffering, she opened herself up. As the circle shattered, she felt the agony of the fire that churned around her, felt all the pain of things remembered and unremembered flow like molten metal through her veins. Arms clutched tight to herself, she sprawled fetal across the searing floor, the mark at her shoulder like a white-hot brand. She felt the stone burning between her fingers, the dagger ready in her other shaking hand.

As the creature's rage consumed the ring that was her last protection, the power that her pain made wrapped around her and exploded out in a pulse of unsurpassed fury.

In her heart, the song of her magic was a single pure note that threaded the shriek of the beast as its flame and its power were consumed.

Then it was over suddenly, and she was on the floor fighting to breathe, the black stone gone from her grasp. In her head, the song had been replaced by another sound that it took her a moment to realize was her own scream, her body convulsing from within like that of the Ilvani she had killed for mercy's sake.

She forced herself to look up. Across from her, she saw the creature rise.

The shroud of blue-black flame was a ravenous storm, the beast shattered and broken within it, dripping black ichor from its joints and its shredded tongue as it screamed. But its bone-talons still rent the marble as it surged toward her, Sharyna rolling, managing to slash out once with the dagger even as the creature broke her shoulder with a lash of its tail and sent the blade spinning from her hand.

It seized her in its smoldering foreclaws, lifted her as if she weighed nothing. Sharyna heard her ribs break, but she was beyond feeling it now. She sprawled helpless in a cocoon of white-hot bone and flesh, feeling the lash of tongue and tail as they bound her tight and the beast's shrieking maw opened wide.

Then from behind the creature, she saw a sudden flash of steel. The spiked tail that held her was severed suddenly, its lifeless flesh releasing her as it opened convulsively and split and turned to ash.

As Sharyna struck the floor, she saw a figure circling. Her own dagger and sword were a blur as they cut deep into the creature's flesh, gouts of black spilling to the air as its life bled away.

She dreamed it was the warrior come back to save her, just for a moment. An uncertain instant before her vision cleared. Then she saw Sanos cut beneath the towering beast as it tried to flee, slashing up through abdomen and spine as he twisted away.

Sharyna saw the creature's eyes flicker to black as it fell, and then there was something at her lips as the clear sweetness she recognized as a healing draught was forced to her tongue.

A cloak was wrapped around her. She thought she saw Sanos watching her from what seemed very far away. She saw nothing after that.

She awoke in the single bed of a narrow attic room, sunlight through grimed glass and the tightness of woolen blankets warm around her.

"Wondered when you'd get back."

As she tried to focus, Sharyna saw Sanos leaning back in a wooden chair at the window, tankard in hand. The visual echo made her blink as she tried to sit up, feeling a stiffness in her arms and legs that threatened to drag her back down again.

There was water in a pitcher at the bedside table, but it took an effort to reach it. Sharyna had to wait for the burning in her throat to subside before she spoke.

"Where..." she tried to say, but a fit of coughing took her.

"The Stone Ear. Tavern. Emond in the kitchen rents the room."

"How long?"

"Near a week, even with the potions I liberated from Andarost's stores."

"You went back?"

Sanos nodded as he let his chair drop. "Took what was light enough to carry and safe enough to hold. I had the others hole up for a while, got them enough coin to see them out of the city. They're scared but they'll do all right."

"Coin won't heal the damage done to them..."

Sanos was silent for a moment. "You should worry for yourself."

"Andarost had no power to hurt me."

"Not what I meant. You don't know what it was, do you?"

Sharyna looked away, shook her head.

"Khimerean," Sanos said. He spat.

Like most had, Sharyna had heard the name before, countless times. In the way Sanos spoke now, though, it carried a taint of foulness she had never felt before, couldn't explain.

"Demons? Creatures of darkness living within the earth? Children's stories."

"Then you heard the one about how such creatures flee from healers' magic? They'll feed on arcane power, suck the mana dry from earth, air, and wizard alike, but the animys of life is toxic to them?"

Sharyna had heard. Fables, she'd always been told. Nightmare creatures from a long-lost age.

"You've seen them before?" All she could think to say.

Sanos was silent a moment. "I saw a lot of things once." He stood, slid the chair away as he stared out at the window. Not wanting to look at her, Sharyna thought. "You think of any other explanation for what that stone let you do that night, for what drained that thing of power to let me cut it down like a slaughterhouse steer and not get killed for my trouble, I'll have it anytime."

At the mention of the stone, Sharyna forced herself upright even as Sanos shook his head. "It's wrapped in my cloak, under the bed. I wouldn't touch the thing. You want my advice, you'll walk away from it."

"I need to know what it is. My order needs to know."

"You should walk away from that order just as fast."

When Sharyna woke the next morning, Sanos was dressed for the road, buttoning a high-collared jacket that hid the brand at his neck. He had a broadsword scabbard strapped to his pack, looked for all the world as if twenty years had fallen from him as he slung it on.

He watched her where she lay. Sharyna waited for him to speak.

"Killing Andarost would have been a lot easier," he said at last. She heard the edge in his voice, remembered his fear at the laboratory door. "Do it as a warning for the next one. Kill them all if you can get that close to them so easy."

"It isn't about warning," she said. "It's about justice."

"Justice for who?"

She remembered her parents then, as she always did. She didn't answer Sanos. He didn't ask again.

He was still there as sleep took her, but when she woke in the morning, he was gone.

It took another three days of rest and Emond sending up a steady supply of hardy soup for her to regain enough strength to wield her blades. That told her it was time to go. It took her no time to pack. Sanos's cloak and a purse of silver argryns he had left her, a set of traveling clothes he'd procured from somewhere, her dagger and sword were all she had to carry.

As she dressed, Sharyna thought she could still see the marks of the moonsign at her shoulder, faint now. Maybe there only in her mind, but she felt a tension twist in her when she touched the amulet before wrapping it tightly, slipping it to the bottom of her pack.

She was alone again, the way it had to be. Each time, though, it got harder.

Most times in the empty aftermath of success, she thought of the warrior who had trained her to the blade, and the ache she wouldn't name would twist through her for a moment, or a day.

This time, she lingered in the room where Sanos had cared for her, and she thought of her father and mother who had died as slaves and never known what strength they had given to the daughter they left behind.

It would take a great deal longer, she knew, for their faces to finally fade.

— Black Run —

HE WAS PAST THE INTERFACE, clear and home, when both port engines blew. The last ghosts of the Black were behind him, the lights of the field ahead, and *Fate's Lady* was an out-of-control missile that shook with the screams of the dead.

The starboard engines howled in protest as Declan twisted the yoke and punched full rudder in a desperate attempt to keep from pitching into a resolutely final dive. The crippled aerocraft lurched as each blast of fire from the port side punched a shockwave through its shuddering frame, Declan answering with power to the starboard engines, the control displays on his console pushed beyond all their half-dozen red lines.

The arc of his descent was fed by a steady pulse of force, the cockpit and Declan within it hammered in relentless waves. Like the impetus cradle he'd seen on Commodore Jessop's desk that first night, the image in his mind suddenly, unbidden. Steel spheres on thin-spun wires, set to striking, back and forth. Transmission of energy, absorbed and reformed, back and again in an endless cycle. *Clack. Clack. Clack.*

Clack.

A sudden fissure traced its way along the cockpit glass. A last tendril of ghost-light had broken off from the cloud behind him, trying to force its way in. The mist had never followed him this far before, never tried to reach him so hard before, shrieking as it split rivets before it was finally snatched away.

Clack.

The steel crate locked up in the cargo well below and behind him was what the ghost-light sought. The power it contained. Through his console, on the spark line at his ears, Declan heard the force held within that crate press gently against weld-sealed panels, against the pressured wall of air within those panels that held it safe. Not a sound of escape sought for. Just a reminder to anyone left to listen that it was there.

Clack.

In his mind and memory, Declan heard the screams of the dead.

Time to fly.

The black steppes they had soared over since liftoff at Rainald had all borne names once, but those names were long burned away by blood and fire and black steel in the Great War That Was. This was where it had ended. The Last Hundred Days, they called it, and Declan had been there. He'd seen much of the destruction first hand, but always from a distance. Soaring high above countless conflagrations in what had passed for aerocraft then, strapping himself into wood and canvas like every other flyboy.

As he watched through the cockpit glass now, the broad grasslands were suddenly gone beneath a bank of cloud that had appeared as if from nowhere. A great sea of mist spread beneath the star-streaked sky, disappearing into shadow at the horizon. Adjusting course, Declan took them up and above it. *Fate's Lady's* four engines were a pulsing roar as they pulled the aerocraft on through the night.

"Sound off." Declan adjusted the set of the audiophone at his mouth, hearing its faint echo through the spark line.

"Lucias, sir."

"Efram, captain."

"Hillard."

"Varn, sir."

The voices sounding out from their posts behind and below and above felt young to him. And despite the fact that two of them had years on him, Declan was reminded of how old he felt. Telling himself he should have let it end. At each launch, the thought worked through him no matter how many other things he needed to focus on, assessing a dozen readings simultaneously from the air console display, matching course to the gridlines of the chart clipped to the navigation panel on his right. Glancing down through the lower cockpit glass to see the endless bank of cloud unfold its seeking fingers toward them.

"Assess stations and report to the cabin for debriefing."

He could have said no the first time. There'd been no orders given, because the war was done and he was finished. A decorated flyboy, mustered out. Risen beyond the reach of orders by the medals at his lapels and the fragments of black iron buried in his chest.

But they had called him back, and he had met with Jessop alone, and the commodore had asked him.

"What will it take for you to fly again?"

As he had each time since he first answered that question, Declan met his crew only at sunset before the Black Run. Alone in the mess that had held two hundred at a meal in the last days of war, he assessed their faces, recognizing only one from a previous sortie. The navigator, Lucias, who drank with the others and laughed more easily than any man who'd made and survived the Black Run should.

The survival rate on the Black Run was the most classified part of all its many secrets. Those who made it were offered escalating double pay for return missions after their first flight, a staggering sum even for top-echelon air corps crews. A few, like Lucias, took it. Most of them, the ones that walked away, Declan never saw again.

He was in his flight leathers, collar up and hat set at an angle. From their perspective, it would no doubt look as though he was making sure his wings caught the light, the red and gold of the master air corps. No higher insignia, no higher station for an aeronaut. However, his larger purpose was to keep the light from his own eyes, letting him watch the others from shadow without them seeing his scrutiny.

They were drinking a lager of the north country that was tapped as black as night and came with a name Declan couldn't pronounce. He drank alongside the four members of his crew as they talked about school years not so long gone, and of gang fights as boys in the cities, and of the war and of missing the glory days of flying, and of their hunger to once again claim what they could of that glory.

Declan laughed with them, and he raised his tankard to a successful mission, but he couldn't taste any of it. The laughter, the faith, the bittersweet burnt darkness of his draught as he drained it. Not anymore.

"What will it take for you to fly again?"

Commodore Jessop had asked the question the night Declan came to him, its answer left hanging as the silver-haired officer stood at a sideboard and swirled ice in a pair of crystal tumblers. The office was paneled in dark oak, its austere lines speaking to the war-room it had once been. Maps of a half-dozen battlegrounds were still pinned to the walls, marked with troop movements and air zones as they'd been in the last days of the Great War That Was. Held there as if someone might simply have called a temporary halt to that great crusade, waiting for the stalled passage of time to start up again.

"The war's done, sir," was what Declan said at last. "War flying's what I do. I don't know that there's a place for me in the air anymore."

"The war's done, yes. But how will it stay done?" Jessop half-filled both tumblers from an unlabeled bottle, its whiskey the deepest nut-brown. "And what should men of war like you and I expect to do in order to keep it done?"

The sideboard stood two perfectly perpendicular paces from the office's desk, to which Jessop returned to set one tumbler at either edge. He brought the bottle with him.

Declan nodded thanks, but he didn't drink at once. He was feeling a weariness, a discomfort at the surroundings, and at the starched dress greys he hated to wear, and at the summons that had brought him here. Not a summons, he had to remind himself. A request to a decorated air captain, mustered out. He was finished, though, and that knowledge gave rise to a dismissive mindset that he could feel occlude the deference that the blue stripes at Jessop's shoulder should have inspired.

The commodore didn't seem to care about any of that. He drank for both of them, nearly draining his tumbler before he set it down again.

"In the midst of history, the ending of one thing becomes the beginning of another." Jessop spoke evenly, as to an equal. "History is a spiral, twisting round past the same points time and time again, but the spiral widens each time. Reflecting what came before, but growing broader. Faster. Out of control."

"I'm afraid I'm not much for analogy, sir."

Commodore Jessop's eyes were pale blue, set behind moon-lensed spectacles that caught the light of the office as a faint sheen of white. He wore dark leather over his dress uniform despite the warmth of the room, its door closed tight and two full-dress guards on the other side of it. The commodore drained his tumbler and filled it again. And as Declan reached for his own drink, he saw the rack of steel spheres for the first time.

The cradle of impetus. He'd seen it before, had heard it called that, but couldn't remember from when or where. A child's toy, he thought. It sat on the desk to Declan's right, and as Commodore Jessop caught the captain's eye settling on the apparatus, he reached for it. A finger pulled the leftmost sphere aside, then let it go. *Clack.* Energy driven through an unmoving medium, transformed to motion that fought against gravity, then was reclaimed. *Clack.*

"The Great War was the last war that will ever be fought on that scale of bloodshed," Jessop intoned impassively. "Or so some say. Because the scope of the war's destruction showed the futility of war. Sixteen millions dead, some say. A conflict priced out in blood and bone. And in the end, none of that will make any difference to stop the next Great War that will be. Do you know why, captain?"

Clack. For the spheres at the end of the cradle, force made movement. For the spheres trapped between them, force was only a pressure to be accepted and channeled and released again. Declan didn't know what answer the commodore wanted, so he simply shook his head.

"Because the dead of the last war have no voice that the living who start the next war will ever hear."

Clack.

Ice against crystal. Declan raised his tumbler, sipping slowly. He tasted black oak and faint spice and a smoothness that spoke to great age. "The politics and purpose of war were never my worry, sir. And I never claimed to understand them."

"Yet you fought all the same. Why is that, captain?"

Eighteen years Declan had on him the first time he went up. He'd lied about his age when he signed on to the mech brigade at sixteen, tall and strong and passing for twenty years without a second glance. Height and muscle were the two things he thanked his father for, or could have thanked him for if he hadn't drank himself to death. The man's towering height and the strength of his hand were all that Declan could remember of him now.

He'd started as a fuel scamp, working the transfer tanks and never knowing that the field corporals had given him the task because of how inherently dangerous it was. When he'd shown the skill to survive that, they put him onto refueling light reconnaissance craft, then the fighters. From there to canvas patching and rivet work, and Declan had begun to take apart engines and rack guns in his off hours. Studying their strange beauty, the transmutation of fire to force and motion. Ratcheting valves and bolts into careful position. *Clack.*

Clack. Orbs of steel swinging across a black desk.

Twenty-one at the war's end and flying for two years, he'd made ace three times over. The Medal of Honor had been pinned to his chest in a ceremony a week after armistice. The quick snap of brass and steel locked to his uniform. *Clack.*

The pinpoint sound of air-stressed rivets ricocheted through *Fate's Lady's* steel frame, sounding out like the striking of intermittent hailstones. *Clack. Clack.*

It wasn't protocol to name aerocraft. Not like the big airships or even the biggest guns of the Great War, whose christenings bestowed a kind of power on them intended to make an enemy know fear. Declan had named all four of his Black Run craft, though, and had buried three of those names so far on the landing field. He did it because he needed to feel like he could count on the aerocraft, as he knew he could count on all his crew. As he knew he would need to.

Clack. In his memory, the sound of burning bullets tearing through the fuselage of his first solo flight, scoping out trench lines with a mapper in the tail gunner's seat. He'd almost dumped that mapper along the convoluted aerial arc that took them up and over the triwing sniper craft that had appeared from nowhere, dropping from the grim halo of a winter sun.

In his memory, the sound of his guns as he returned fire, taking the sniper out. *Clack*. Time slowing down as arcs of bright fire touched out and shredded the flag-tattoos of its wings, its tail, as it spiraled for the ground.

Declan never answered the commodore's second question that night. Why fight a war he hadn't understood? But in the dark-paneled office, watching the motion of steel spheres, he responded to the first question with a question of his own.

"Why do you want me to fly again?"

The commodore leaned down. Declan heard the sound of a key in a deep-set lock. *Clack*. Then a drawer of the desk opened with a faint hiss that spoke to it having been air-sealed. Maximum security. Jessop pulled forth a red folder, its seal marked *HIGH TOP SECRET* and broken.

Three words across its face. *THE BLACK RUN*.

"I want you to fly again, Captain Declan, because you're the best air-warrior to have survived four years of carnage that have no precedent in the history of warfare. Possibly the best even counting those who didn't make it back. And I have reports from half a hundred engineers and aeronauts and mechs who tell me that the Black Run can't be flown. I need you to prove them wrong."

Fate's Lady was an aerocraft the like of which had never been seen in the skies of the Great War That Was. A new design in the aftermath of that conflict, and the work of air corps engineers who could focus exclusively on better ways to fly now that they had no more need to design better ways to kill.

In its shape could be seen the lines of the last Great War bombers, but *Fate's Lady* and its lost predecessor craft had their bomb gear stripped out for Declan's missions. He'd made five sorties in the new craft so far. Twenty-two runs in total over the past two years, each testing the aerocraft's design in ways its makers could never have anticipated.

Her frame was riveted alloy steel, her canvas reinforced with tempered oak slats along all the length of her wedge-shaped wings and raised tail, all cutting the air like matched cleavers. The cockpit was swept forward, guns mounted fore and aft, over and under for an all-around fire zone. Even with the cable crane and the triple-sealed cargo space that had replaced the bomb bay, the craft was built for a speed that the best fighter craft of the Great War would have had trouble matching. Its engines were tight twins set close in on the wings, resolutely churning black sky as they vented trails of smoke behind them.

"Captain! All on deck and reporting."

Lucias's voice on the spark line drew Declan's attention from the mist-wall and the night beyond, his gaze alighting on the mirror above the cockpit glass. In its reflection, he had a view back into the narrow cabin and its single bench. Efram, Hillard, and Varn were squeezing in on that bench now, plugging into the spark line that carried voice to ear over the thrumming howl of the engines. Lucias sat across from them in the navigator's seat. All of them were watching their captain, waiting. Locked to his gaze in the mirror as he caught the wary eye of each in turn.

"The information I'm about to impart to you is need to know." Declan's tone was impassive through the spark line, the engines and the hiss of air across the wings a fierce and constant storm. The words came from memory with a too-easy familiarity, repeated at the beginning of each Black Run, twenty-two times before. A mix of crew each time, but always including new recruits who had no idea as to the scope and darkness of their mission until it was underway.

"By special dispensation of air corps command and Commodore Jessop, you are all hereby assigned special intelligence rank blue-one, clearing you for the receipt of top secret information from intelligence command-grade officers. Including me."

A faint groan twisted through *Fate's Lady,* resonating within the fuselage. Through the glass, Declan saw fingers of cloud reaching up from the mist-wall. Seeking. Still barely more than intangible, but strong enough to set the aerocraft's steel skeleton humming. He saw the looks of uncertainty on the faces of the three new crew.

"The destruction of the Last Hundred Days was the worst of the

Great War," Declan continued. "Two millions dead, with casualty rates of ninety percent. Survivors with eyes burned out and driven mad, screaming for the medicos to kill them. Official reports from the army intelligence corps drafted at the time assessed the destruction as the result of the unlimited use of toxic and infectious munitions in the last days of conflict, in violation of treaty and the articles of war."

On the console beside him, Declan saw the outside temperature begin to tick downward. A sudden hiss of sound like passing hail enveloped them, loud even over the spark line earpieces. Efram looked up, the young mech flinching as the sound shivered into resonance with the drone of the engines. The gunners Varn and Hillard, Lucias the navigator, all kept their eyes tight to Declan's, who saw in them a reflection of the darkness in his own gaze.

They were halfway across the mist-wall and through the unseen Black below, finishing the first leg of the crossing over a day's-march worth of burned-out landscape and sealed airspace that no civilian had passed through in nearly five years.

"Special operations units surveying the battlefield in the aftermath of armistice determined that the destruction of the Last Hundred Days was, in fact, caused not by bombardment, but by unknown forces that had been unearthed and triggered by bombardment. Pockets of energy and power, of unknown origin, found at the epicenter of destruction. Power beyond anything heretofore known to any military or government."

"Sir?" The front gunner Hillard had a nervous tick that manifested as a clicking stammer. "What manner of..."

"It's arcana, son," Lucias called out with a grin. "Magic. The forces of the black arts on the battlefield..."

Declan cut him off with a dark glare, but it didn't still the navigator's knowing smile. Lucias pulled a red-foldered mission map from his console with a flourish. He broke its seal, *HIGH TOP SECRET,* then withdrew and unfolded it across the knees of the other three where they huddled close across from him.

"Intelligence branch has name-classified this power source as the Black Force," Declan said, "and its true nature remains unknown. We're here to bring it home."

"What do you believe in, captain?"

Across the dark desk from Commodore Jessop, Declan was scanning the contents of the red folder. Maps and intelligence reports, detailing an unknown energy. A thing that the explorers and engineers who discovered it had named the Black Force. "I believe in doing my job, sir."

"But that job ended with the end of the Great War. You and I, every other aeronaut and commander, all face the same fate in the aftermath of battle. What will any of us do now?"

"Find something else to believe in." Declan read carefully through force schematics, complex breakdowns of numbers and variables. Hypothetical figures that made no sense. Force and motion, transmutation of energy. Though he understood the mechanics of the formulae, their resolution was beyond him.

The commodore's tumbler was full again, the ice melting down and sounding out faintly against crystal. "Do you believe in the arcane, captain? And I ask this question most seriously."

Declan sipped again at his own drink, tasting more water than whiskey now. His hand was shaking. "You mean like in fairy stories, sir? The Anórà caravaners, telling your future or talking to your grandmother's shade at carnival time?"

"I mean the mystical, son. The unknown. Real arcana, not sleight of hand or parlor games. Forces unexplained, mind over matter. Messages passing from mind to mind, from the future or the grave. The dead walking again."

In Jessop's even tone, Declan heard a caution that slowed the retort already on his lips. He looked up from the pages before him, holding the pale gaze steady behind their bright lenses.

"Tell me why I should, sir," he said instead.

The three new crew took the rest of Declan's briefing without question. No queries on the particulars of the contact. The hook drop, the pickup. Full battle stations for the flight out. The crews for the Black Run were picked for their ability to absorb a plan and follow it through. They'd been pulled from across the air corps, from a dozen different squadrons. All men, like Declan, aware that when the war ended, they had lost something.

Only in their eyes did he see any hint of the profound fear he knew was there.

"Sir." The tail gunner, Varn, was a quiet man from what Declan had seen of him in the mess. A half-dozen confirmed kills according to the dossier he'd reviewed, before a bullet to the chest took him out of commission. "This flight was categorized at risk level red before we all signed on. Besides the speed and the fact we've got nowhere to land in an emergency, what's the risk in a remote cable snatch?"

Declan caught Lucias's smirk again. "The power in the Black Force attracts like to like." As he said it, the captain heard the echo of Jessop speaking the same words to him when it all started. "The unknown to the unknown. The dead haunt the Black. The battlefields below, the clouds above. Every flyboy that fell from the air here. Every balloon sent up and shot down, every fighter, bomber, every surveillance craft. They fly the mist-wall. They're already below us, but even up here, we feel them. Once we make our pickup, they'll be on us. They'll want our cargo. They'll come through us to get it."

A trace flared at Lucias's console, sounding out through the spark line. The echoing ping of a short-range signal warning. "Sky tower is online. Hook is in the air and shining bright."

"We get them first. Simple as that." Declan's gaze was off the mirror and back to his console even before the others broke from the cabin to scramble for their own posts. "Combat stations."

He brought them down from the star-bright sky through the haze of cloud that never broke above the Black. The mist-wall, the explorer corps had called it. "That fog never lifts," Commodore Jessop had told him. "The wind tears at it, the rains hammer it, but it hangs there like a shroud just the same. And a lucky thing as far as you're concerned. Traveling over it, you'll feel only the faintest traces of anomalous activity. Then a fast descent for the pickup. Then out."

"And how am I expected to hit a pickup at dive speed? In the dark and under fog? Sir?" At the commodore's desk, Declan had stared at the carefully scribed charts that showed what purported to be the safe routes in across the Black, a sky tower site sitting at their webbed center like a dark spider.

"You've made steeper descents than that in your day. I watched one, in fact. Wat Aerodrome, when you were hit. I was there for that landing. Or whatever you might call it."

At Wat, Declan had been flying a crippled bomber back from the trench lines on one engine, venting fire that was rapidly draining his tanks with no way to shut down. He'd had to climb at a hard bank to keep the fire from spreading and setting the crippled aerocraft alight, a task made more daunting by the iron shards of his shattered second engine burning white-hot below his heart.

He was within sight of the aerodrome when he finally ran dry, dropping to the field below in a screaming dive that was the only warning he could give to clear the runway. He hit clean on the first bounce, but things had gone shadowy after that. Declan's next memory from that flight was of coughing up blood while carrying his bombardier out of the wreckage. The other man hadn't made it.

That night in the commodore's office, Declan had said nothing in response to Jessop's words or the memories. He just sipped from his drink again, which had been refilled from the commodore's bottle without him noticing.

The heroes of that red folder were the explorers and sappers of the Black, who worked underground always, never exposing themselves to the screams of the dead that scoured the battlefields above. Even before he heard that scream for the first time himself, Declan felt it, in cramped handwritten reports detailing the first disastrous attempts of the explorer corps to make open crossings across those fields.

The sappers had gone underground in the aftermath, cutting deep warrens beneath a roof of rock and earth to search for the Black Force that the explorers had first uncovered. They came and went from the battlefield by way of tunnels that had taken half a year to cut. Four years of trench fighting had made it all too easy, digging and clearing and mapping out sources of Black Force that would sound out across a spark signal. The unknown power that had laid waste to the battlefields of the Last Hundred Days, imposing final silence on the guns of war but filling earth and air with the screams of two million dead.

Where Declan drove *Fate's Lady* earthward now, the sky tower rose within the mist-wall's eternal cloud. The only point of real elevation in the shattered black landscape below, it was set above the sapper warrens' only external access point within the Black. Those entry tunnels were blocked by multiple redundant doorways of cold-rolled steel, held fast with reverse-pressure deadlocks and magnetite bolts.

When Declan and his crew got their call, it meant that the sap-rats of the warrens had unsealed those doors one by one for the passage of a single steel crate. It would be winched along a last shaft, set into position beneath the tower, and then cable-lifted to the black sky.

Declan didn't think on what those crates held. Not his business. But the brief hints he had seen in Jessop's red folder that first night spoke of tangible forces, night-black and roiling like liquid metal, moved and contained within fields of pressured air. Pulleys and relay gears, wire-controlled from the dark bunkers beneath the tower, would set that dark cargo into place atop the tower. A secondary remote would detonate the release charge on an attached canister balloon, letting it lift on a tether of spun cable to hang a shining beacon hook in the white-cloud sky.

As *Fate's Lady* cut through that cloud, Declan's cockpit glass began to flare with a shimmering of silver light. He adjusted throttle carefully to keep pace with the rising speed of the dive, the relative quiet of the inbound run giving way suddenly to shrieking voices. Tendrils erupted from the surrounding white, and then all around the aerocraft was a writhing storm of spectral movement.

The screaming of the dead slammed through the fuselage like the pounding of some unearthly fist, a shudder following in its wake as the temperature display crashed and a wisp of white vapor congealed across the console's glass panels. Declan was too focused to feel the sudden snap of cold, but he could see his breath freezing in the air before him. He heard an edge of panic in Efram's voice as he called out.

"Outside atmosphere at the cargo post! Possible breach!"

"Negative." Lucias cut the young mech off with a laugh. "We're whole, full speed, and right side up even. This is contact."

And just like that, the skies around *Fate's Lady* were alive with ghost-light. Streams of radiance pulsed in at the observation glass, the domes of the gun turrets lit up in silver and white. A squadron of spectral fighters had materialized high on the starboard side, their stepped wings shattered and streaming canvas, torn and flapping like shredded flesh.

"Fuck my eyes..." Through the spark lines, Hillard's voice was tight with fear.

"Cut chatter," Declan said in return. "Fire at will."

The guns barked like hunting hounds held too long at the chain, and all around *Fate's Lady*, the air was torn to white and red fire. The spectral fighters shuddered under the onslaught, the aeronauts at their controls mercifully lost within a nimbus of light. No bodies to be seen. Only vague shapes of mist and bone that streamed and rippled as they flashed past and were gone.

"Cargo," Declan barked. "Status."

"Visual made! Line away!" Where the cargo console was mirrored at the cockpit controls, Declan watched Efram punch the winch to send a snare line from the belly of the aerocraft to the haze of white below. The cargo hold was sealed from the inside, the mech working remote by touch-cable and the needle displays before him.

The captain watched the distance readouts and the faint marker of the sky tower signal mirrored on his own console as he fought to keep *Fate's Lady* on course. He could see the tower beacon now, but he could also see a fast-moving triwing fighter tacking toward him, coming in close as it unleashed traces of spectral fire.

"Front guns, clear the course! Tower dead ahead!" This close to the catch, Declan had no room to maneuver. His first flight out, he'd had to bank hard on his approach to escape the attention of three ghostly guncraft that appeared to have slammed together in the crash that took them out. They had flown in that formation still, locked tight and twisting, spitting fire from every direction at once in a caustic cloud.

Declan had needed to make three passes for the catch on that fateful first run. Never since. He wasn't planning on having that change tonight.

The staccato roar of Hillard's front gun sent tremors through the canvas and steel of the cockpit, cold-iron bullets spitting across the sky in a broad swath that swept through the triwing as it rolled. The ghostly craft shuddered and shredded and unfurled away into the vapor of the mist-wall once more. The twinned blades of *Fate's Lady's* engines chopped it to slivers of white as Declan took them through.

The explorers who first mapped the sappers' course through skewed tunnels beneath charred battlefields had tried to take the Black Force out through those same tunnels once. Only once. No one in the transport team had been left alive to confirm the attack, but when the search team found what was left of them, it was clear that the spirits of battlefield and trench above and around could find their way into the new-cut tunnels easily enough. The ghosts of the Black were drawn to the power captured in those steel crates. The Black Force could be tracked and located, tagged and studied. It could be constrained and carefully moved, but only so long as it stayed out of the awareness of the dead it had destroyed.

By careful and costly trial, the sap-rats had determined that moving the Black Force in its specialized containment to the deep foot of the sky tower held no risk. By cable and air-driven conveyer, each crate was shifted and lifted without the touch of mortal hands, the power within seemingly sensitive to the presence of the living in a way still not wholly understood. From the tunnels to the top of the sky tower was a slow process of remote transit, but one that somehow eluded the preternatural awareness of the dead.

Getting the crates from the tower to the security of the aerodrome beyond the mist-wall, away from the ghosts who would kill to retrieve it, was Declan's job.

"This will be the most dangerous run you've ever made," Jessop had told him that first night. "Chances are, you won't make it out."

Declan had said nothing for a long while, staring at navigation charts and notes, the Black and its mist-wall laid out from the red folder like an itemized itinerary of doom. Then he spoke.

"When do I go up, sir?"

Time to fly.

"Contact!" Declan saw Efram's console report the catch as the sky tower flashed past beneath them. Even against the power of the engines at three-quarter throttle, he felt the lurch as their cargo was lofted into the air beneath them. The grinding roar of the winch engines sounded out as the steel crate was hauled in.

The catch line was an ungainly mess of cable, thick-wrapped and resisting all but the most concerted attempts to coil it cleanly. But its misshapen form had a specific purpose, with each spiraling strand of that cable shaped of cold-rolled steel that the first explorers of the Black had determined could keep the specters of the dead landscape at bay.

"Locked!" Efram called. "Hold sealed!"

"Full speed!" Declan throttled up, the rising pulse of the engines threading through *Fate's Lady's* frame as she climbed.

He took them above the eternal cloud to improve line of sight beneath the star-streaked sky, but the relative quiet that had marked their incoming approach was shattered by the tempest of white light that followed them now. Waves of mist rose up to all sides, splitting into spectral storm-light that erupted as the shades of a hundred air battles all fought at once.

"Fire at will," Declan said evenly, but the guns were already blazing, their report hammering through *Fate's Lady's* steel frame like matched waves. His hands and feet were locked to the controls, the measured snap of slats and rudder driving them on. *Clack. Clack.*

To all sides, lost fighter squadrons resolved into semisolid form, laying down strafing fire that Declan rolled over and around as the wings trembled with the strain. Ahead, a spectral haze of balloons vented flame and smoke, burning as they had when they fell from the sky, but ever-unconsumed in this silver night. He tacked down and under them, broadening the field of fire of the aerocraft as he rolled, and trusting that the expertise of his gunners would take advantage of it.

He lost track of the number of craft he saw shred away to silver mist. He stopped watching to see how quickly they would reform, knowing that the speed of *Fate's Lady* would outdistance the dead as they struggled across the sky. What was behind them was no worry. Above and below, coming in from the side was where Declan focused. Straight ahead along the next twisting leg of the course whose adjustments Lucias passed up to him as scribbled notes.

"You know what I think?" Lucias's voice was loud on the spark line, Declan catching a quick mirror-glimpse of the excited navigator in the jump seat behind him.

"I don't remember asking," the captain said as he watched the slow yaw of a burning guncraft to starboard. As with many of the craft that pursued them, its own ghost-guns were silenced. Neither Declan nor the intelligence operatives who dissected the details of each mission had yet discerned the laws that governed the forms these crippled craft could take. There was no rhyme or reason to which particular instance of a craft's final minutes was chosen for its deadly resurrection. The guncraft was trying to ram them, double arcs of fire tracing out from Hillard and Varn at fore and aft as *Fate's Lady* rolled. The gunners' chatter was clipped, each marking sightings in the other's blind spots. Declan took it all in, feeling the fight around him beyond what he could sense of it through the glass.

"This arcana they talk about." Lucias was flipping charts, checking speed and fuel marks as he did. "This magic, it's not of this world."

"There's a lot of things in this world you and I have never seen."

As if in response to Declan's statement, a pulse of silver lightning flared beyond the port observation glass. A jagged line of cloud unfolded there, opening like a wound to disgorge a full fighter wing. Their lines were tantalizingly familiar, but as hard as he tried, Declan couldn't recognize the ghost ships of the Black. Something about their spectral shapes seemed to defy his eye, so that he had no idea whether these might once have been his own flyboys trying to kill him now. He sent *Fate's Lady* into a hard starboard roll, the engines whining as gravity fed their power.

"Look up and around, captain. The night sky full of stars, full of other worlds. Other places beyond this one. Other times, even. Think on the fighters our boys flew at the start of the war, then compare them to the *Lady*, here. Think of what they'll be building ten years from now, or a hundred. This Black Force could be the power of a people more advanced than us. Or of the future, sent back through time."

"Then what's with the ghosts of years past trying to kill us?"

"Movement from the future breaks the past, maybe. Sets up ripples in time."

In front of him, Declan saw a bomber airship suddenly coalesce from a bright storm of mist. It was huge and it was burning, venting black gas and molten steel. Its dozens of frayed rope lines shimmered beneath it like dark tentacles, reaching for them. He heard a shout from Hillard in the nose beneath him, but even as the guns barked, they were too close. Declan punched down, feeling the shudder as *Fate's Lady* went full slats-out, wings and tail clawing the air. Hard on the yoke took them into a controlled fall, then back out again, the spectral tendrils passing over and across.

On the spark line, someone screamed.

"Sound off," Declan called. He pulled up straight, one gun still sounding out but no sense of who was firing.

"Lucias, clear."

"Clear, sir. Efram, sir."

"Hillard, clear."

No word from Varn at the tail guns. Then a choked voice. "Varn, hit sir. A white light, like some kind of whip… Mother of fuck…"

"Fight it, gunner. Full speed and fire."

The last maneuver had taken them off the course of safe lines that Declan had seen scribed on Jessop's map that first night. Mission after mission since the first, he had gained a faith in that complex web of courses and coordinates like nothing he'd ever believed in before. Lucias was already passing up corrected numbers, Declan watching the set of the console's needles as he adjusted. He pushed them toward an opening ahead, both guns pounding again. Full speed and flat slats, the foot pedals punched down to the floor. *Clack.*

The deep dark of night was the safest time to make the Black Run. *The quietude,* a half-dozen pages of the red folder's intelligence had ironically called it, explaining all the observations and the guesswork behind that view. All the possible yet still unknown reasons why that particular time could slow the ghosts of the black in their murderous rage. Give the mission at least a fighting chance.

That first mission, aerocraft and crew limping back from the battlefields of the Black, all anyone at the aerodrome would have heard from the heart of the quietude was Declan screaming.

He had named the aerocraft of that maiden mission *First Star*, thinking on the act of a child's wishing upon the first signs of night. What was left of *First Star* had dropped to the landing field at the end of that night as a ball of crimson flame. The barrage of fire from the Black's ghost fleet had stripped away the cladding from most of the left wing, the shrieking voices of the dead twisting across open air into cockpit and cabin. A sound of madness that burned in the mind whether the spark wire was live or not.

Declan thought he'd heard his navigator scream back to the ghosts on that disastrous flight. But he was dead when they pulled the wreckage apart, and Declan had no way to ask if or why he'd done it. Only thinking on it later, he wondered whether the navigator had died in the air, the scream a signal that he had joined the squadrons of the dead. Declan had lost crew in the air since then, but he'd never heard the scream again. He still wondered.

He couldn't remember the navigator's name. In the shock and immediate aftermath of that deadly first landing, it had left him and never returned.

Declan was the only one who had walked away from that first flight. Jessop had met him in the aftermath for a sullen debriefing, the captain sitting at the desk again, the commodore's words a faint blur in his mind. He remembered recounting the flight, the three passes it had taken to make the catch. The damage they had taken in that protracted approach, and how it had slowed their escape.

Commodore Jessop had been curt but not dismissive. Not bothering to hide his surprise that Declan had made it back at all, nor his gratitude that at least a single survivor could tell him what had gone wrong, those responses dutifully written down, one after the other.

But when the commodore told him he was dismissed pending reassignment, Declan had surprised them both.

"No, sir."

Jessop had been standing at his office window, staring out through rippled glass to where the fire was still burning on the field. The room was dark, a single lamp at the desk setting Declan into a pool of silver-white light.

Jessop looked back, appraising him for a long moment. "Captain?"
"When do I go up? Sir?"

Clack.
"What do you believe in, captain?"
Clack.

Rivets were popping on the frame of the cockpit glass from the course Declan carved through the shrouded sky. *Fate's Lady* was rebuilt before each mission by the best mechs and engineers in the corps, all of them selected with the same care as the crews of the Black Run. He could feel the strain of full-speed flight all the same, though. A tremor passed again through the aerocraft's steel frame, pushing back to front, front to back, two waves curling past and through each other.
Clack.

In Jessop's office that first night, the impetus cradle had slowed. Motion lost to inertia, converted to energy of sound.
Clack.
"In the midst of history, the ending of one thing becomes the beginning of another," the commodore said. "The Great War was supposed to end war. Break the old ways, the old treaties. Make it so all nations possessed the memory of what total destruction looks like, preventing any one of them from seeking that destruction again."

Declan reached out for the slowing cradle, letting the uptick of a moving sphere break against his finger and stop to sudden silence.

"But the dead of the last war have no voice that the living who start the next war will ever hear," he said to the commodore. "And all that are left are men who don't know anything but war. People like you and me. Sir."

Declan drained his glass this time, but Jessop made no motion to refill it as it was set back down to the desk. The captain looked up to the pale blue eyes, and as he did, he realized that he had yet to see the commodore blink. Just staring, patient.

"A power never before seen," the commodore said. "Unknown to engineering and mortal knowledge. A beginning that has no end. Our obligation is to ensure that we control the power with which the next Great War will be fought. Our obligation is to understand the Black Force. And my question to you, captain, is what will it take for you to fly again?"

Clack.

With a flick of his finger, Declan let the silver sphere loose to send its momentum into the cradle once more. Transformation of force, cycling without end.

Clack.

A steel shudder rang through the port wing as a lurching roll took them through the narrowest possible corridor within a flotilla of fighters. Their front fire traced out white lines that swirled like a swarm of frost-kissed leaves on a winter wind.

"Corridor clear and counting down," Lucias called out across the spark line. "Breaking the Black and homeward bound." The navigator let out of whoop of triumph that Declan could hear even through the open air. The booming thunder of the front guns swept over and starboard, clearing out the last pursuit. They were approaching the interface, the cloud roiling ahead of them, battering and recoiling against the endless night.

Clack. The port wing sounded out again.

Then Lucias's laugh turned to a sudden scream, as the navigator and the fuselage against which he sat were torn through cleanly by a hundred pulsing traces of ghost-white light.

Declan could feel his hands on the controls, but their movement was entirely instinctive. He pulled *Fate's Lady* into a hard dive to port, craning back to the upper cockpit glass to see the fighter squadron that had materialized above them. The black night was alive with light as ghostly fire pounded them. A cacophony of voices came through the spark line, but he couldn't focus on them.

He could only hear the scream that Lucias made. A scream that wouldn't stop though the navigator's eyes stared lifeless to the console before him, no air drawn from dead lungs.

Declan took them down, hurtling toward the dying edge of mist-wall for the cover it might give him. He prayed for answering fire from the rear guns, but aside from the roar of the engines, *Fate's Lady* was silent now.

"Sound off."

Nothing.

"Varn. Efram. Hillard, sound off."

Over the empty hiss of the spark line, the voices of the other three joined Lucias in the scream that had no end.

Then suddenly, silence. Silence and starlight, and Declan's hands on the controls were shaking as he realized he'd made it through the mist-wall and into empty sky beyond.

He was past the interface, clear and home, when both port engines blew. The last ghosts of the Black were behind him, the lights of the field ahead.

Time to fly.

The approach to Rainald Aerodrome cut a burning swath across the black night, and through most of it, Declan's only thought was of how breathtaking it must have looked from the ground.

He was at full throttle and nose up, hearing the wings groan, pushed to the breaking point, but knowing that nothing else would keep enough air beneath them to carry him in. He ran the landing checklist by dull memory, feeling the wheels drop and lock as he spiraled down from the black sky.

Clack.

Transfer of energy. He braked with full slats and the last of his engines as he hit.

Clack.

He heard the shriek of steel as stanchions and frame slammed up from the aerocraft's belly. Then Declan was airborne and separated from the wreck, the nose and cockpit sheered off from the fuselage as it tore apart behind him. The wedge-shaped wings folded in on themselves, the last of the fuel fountaining out in a red-black arc as tanks blew, fixed in the white gleam of evenlamps along the field's edge. Then that fountain erupted as a scything pulse of elemental flame, cutting through the wreckage like a butcher's blade.

Declan saw support teams swarm out across the field as he pulled himself from what was left of the command seat. He was a hundred paces away from the wreck but had no memory of landing. His thoughts were remarkably clear. Focused in a way that made him understand how wholly unnatural that clarity was.

A wall of water rose up around the flaming wreckage as dousing crews closed in. Medicos came in behind them, circling in the vain hope of seeking survivors. Two of those broke off from the main pack, coming toward him. He waved them off.

"Captain Declan reporting four crew dead. Lucias, Efram, Hillard, Varn, all killed in flight. Tell the rescue teams to fall back." But even as he turned away, he realized that his hand was cut. A gash across his palm where the shattering cockpit glass must have caught him. He hadn't felt it.

He stared down. His thoughts were remarkably clear.

Declan didn't think on what the black crates held. Not his business. But within the wound on his hand, where a slow seepage of blood should have been, he recognized the night-black fluid pulsing there, roiling like liquid metal.

He couldn't smell the fire, he realized. He looked up to see the elemental conflagration a hundred paces away, sending black smoke to scour the stars, but there was no scent of it on the air. No sense of its heat on his face.

When he looked back down to his hand, the wound had closed.

He hadn't felt the frigid cold of the plunge down into the mist-wall, with the dead coming up to meet them. He remembered it from his first Black Run, though, just as he remembered the heat of the fire as the *First Star* had touched down and unwrapped around him like a cocoon of canvas and steel.

The black lager at the mess. He couldn't taste it any more. Couldn't feel the laughter.

Clack.
Footsteps behind him, faint against the roar of flame.
Clack. Clack.

That first Black Run, that disastrous flight, he'd been screaming all the way in. And from when he hit, he remembered the splintering sound that was the triple-sealed cargo hold releasing its crate.

He remembered the shadow that washed across him as he died that night. Remembered it unfurling from its web of pressure and shattered cold-rolled steel to envelop him, to slip inside him and disappear.

He remembered waking again where his body had been thrown clear of the wreckage. Rising to walk away.

"Chances are, you won't make it out," Jessop had said. And he'd been right.

•

Clack.

"Captain Declan."

He turned to see the commodore approach, slowing a half-dozen paces away. He nodded in greeting. He couldn't speak, but the words came all the same.

"When do I go up? Sir?"

Behind the moon-lensed spectacles that caught the dance of fire-light, Jessop's pale blue eyes blinked this time.

"Second time lucky, captain. But luck like yours is bound to run out sometime."

Declan turned toward the line of lighting poles at the edge of the landing field, staring into the darkness beyond to drink in the familiar emptiness there. He felt the pull of that darkness, as he felt the pull of the Black, unseen behind him.

"No, sir. I believe in doing my job, sir."

Our obligation is to understand the Black Force. He remembered Jessop's words with perfect clarity, focused against the shadow that was all the thought and memory lost to him now.

And Declan recognized the importance of that obligation. Because he alone understood how important it was for the Black Force to understand them in return.

The darkness beyond the evenlamps was brightening as the wind tore the smoke away, showing the light of the night sky full of stars, full of other worlds.

"When do I go up, sir?"

— The Voice —

ARDA STARES TO THE FIRE as Silla screams, the blade of his knife stirring gruel in the blackened steel pot. His hand slows at the sound. The smoke of the brazier rises to gently trace grime at his fingertips as the knife slips to rest at the edge of the pot, which he sets aside, away from the heat. Then he rises, walking to the second room as quietly as he knows how. Through the narrow crack of the canvas that blocks the uneven doorway, he looks.

Inside, the crystal-witches have the pallet on the floor. Silla's movements have dislodged the linen and the blankets they bring to wrap her with. He watches as one of the women holds her hands, another with a white-knuckle grip on her shoulders, pressing down with a gentle firmness. That second woman bends close to whisper, her words lost beneath a cry of pain. Arda hears the third woman curse as she works.

Candlelight plays across them from the corners of the room, and Arda presses close to the hairline glow. Scattered life-shards are spread long and thin and bright on a bloodstained shawl, their pulsing glow betrayed by flecks of red. He watches as the hands of the three women drift across the glowing crystals, the prayer of intervention passing from one whisper to the next. He sees hands press down to Silla's forehead, to her legs, to the shadow below her slackened belly as she weeps.

She is silent by the time they leave. The first of the women carries the dark bundle of their work wrapped tight in a tattered blanket. Arda does not ask them as to the stillborn babe's final fate.

As the others slip through the doorway without a word, the third woman steps close to him. She fixes him with cold eyes, brown like winter leaves. She levels words that Arda does not hear, because he watches the gleam of the life-shard in her hand, clutched tight to pulse blood-red between callused fingers. Its glow catches Silla's unmoving form, the cloak that she and Arda use as a blanket wrapped tight around her now.

Arda forces himself to focus. He hears the woman talking, realizes that her words are for him.

"You wait too long," she says, words lashed tight with anger. "You knew the last time, and before that, this isn't for her. The gods' voices whisper our fate to each of us, and hers is not to nurture, nor to ask why."

He looks down on her from a height that nearly touches the lintel of the scarred door, one foot scuffing absently at long-faded marks of arcane fire across the floor. Scars in the stone that never fade. Sometime before he and Silla found their way into this corner of the warren ruins, the Ilvanghlira had cleared out the remnants of whoever lived there before them.

"She cannot do it again," the woman hisses. "She has lost too much, too many times. You spill your seed in her, she feels the child wither within her again, and each time, you leave her an emptiness that only darkness will fill."

This is home. Arda found this space for them, secret and hidden in the ruins that rise like a crumbling wall around the Fastness. It took the power of an artificer to mend the crumbled stones of the door and weave strength back into its aging oak planks. Arda bartered the repairs against the time the wiry arcanist spends with Silla in the shadows when he is done.

"Silla will be all right," Arda says carefully.

With all the coldness in her, the woman curses softly, controlled. At a flick of her fingers, the crystal comes up, exposed and razor-sharp, hovering an inch from Arda's throat. He isn't afraid.

"It should be you next time," she whispers. "You on your back with the life drawn from you. You with your spirit cleaved by the rites."

Arda watches the crystal as it is slipped away. He pays the woman with a chain of silver that his mother once wore. The woman checks its worth with a wave of her fingers, the faint twist of spellcraft turning the metal to a white glow for a moment. It costs him extra for the three of them to come to Silla this late, ranging out beyond the storm-wall after dark. By the time Arda set out to find them, Silla was too far gone to walk.

Without a word, the woman steps out with the others into the chill of the wind-torn rubble. Arda watches them go, then pushes hard to shut and bar the door.

At the brazier, a thin skin covers the gruel. Oats and barley mostly, and one of the dried apples Arda traded for in the market when he sought to find the crystal-witches. He slices it in carefully, then he stirs slowly, steam warming his hands.

He fills a bowl and takes it to Silla with bread. Through the canvas at the second room, open now, she lies on her side, her back to him.

She holds the tattered cloak close around her, shivering in the shadow where planks and canvas are tacked tight across the window.

Arda calls to her, showing her what he has made as he bends low to place it close on the floor. Around her shoulders, the narrow rise of her hips, the cocoon of cloak tightens. She shakes her head.

"Eat," he tells her. "I made it for you." He rises up. He stands and watches her.

Silla turns her head slowly. From under the tangled web of hair, she watches with wet eyes, blinking as Arda turns and leaves. From behind him, he hears her stir.

He tends the fire, feeding dried dung and bits of coal to the shimmering flame. He checks the bar at the door, listens to hear distant shouts beyond, unintelligible. A scream rings out in the distance. He turns away.

When he has given Silla enough time, he goes back. Her eyes are closed. The bowl is empty. He scrapes it carefully to clean it, tracing cracks in the clay with a blunted fingernail. Then he stands at the clear window of the first room and watches a trace of snow brush clouded glass. He studies the familiar view, black sky and black stone touching where tangled ruins flank the road. The gloom lessens farther along the rubble line, where the light of the Fastness fights with a rising Clearmoon, waning but still bright. Outlined within the haze of fire and moon's-light, the battered walls of the ruined temple rise within the swirling shadow that is the storm-wall, marking the edge of the Fastness beyond.

Arda wouldn't have known it was a temple from just those distant lines of its stone shell, but he walked through the grounds one night in search of firewood. He saw what remains of the altar within the shattered walls, the statues of the old gods. They had needed wood then, because it was before he had gained the brazier in trade for the bow and quiver his father left him. He had known he wasn't going to need them anymore because he and Silla found their place to stay. He and Silla found home.

From the first room's window, the firelight lines of the Fastness are the closest landmarks, but he likes to look to the fallen black columns beyond that, marking where the temple once stood. It is busy in the Fastness in a way he does not like. When they went to the thronging settlement to barter for the brazier, Arda let Silla wander from stall to stall in the markets. He saw her smile as she took it all in. They watched the mage duels within the great stone circle around which the

Fastness spread, then ate real meat from a trapper's stall, and Silla had her fortune told by a seer. Arda paid with the last of his copper, but the seer gave it back to him. Then she gave Silla a sliver of sugar-candy, and whispered things to her that she would not let Arda hear.

When they left, Arda told Silla they weren't going back. "It's safer in the warren," he says now to the sleeping Silla, to himself, repeating the words. "We're safer at home." Through the weathered glass, he looks down to see twisting track and laneway meet in the ruins. Rough dirt to one side, grey-black beneath a sheen of dead ice. To the other side, shattered cobblestones spread, the color of the daytime sky. No way for anyone to approach unseen.

Arda speaks out loud, only to himself. "It's late," he says. He watches the sky for snow. "She should rest," he says.

At the door, he checks the bar again. He listens to the faint echo of wind shimmering against the moss-stuffed cracks of the stone wall. He stands at the first room's window again, watching, hoping that the silence of the world outside keeps up. He knows she is sleeping.

He hears our voice then.

Arda looks up, pulling his eyes from the shadowed glass. Silence now. Then again. A quiet whisper. The sound of soft and unshod feet.

In the second room, the window has lost its glass so he covers it against the cold. But from below, he and Silla hear voices. Drifters slipping through from the Fastness sometimes, hoping to pass in safety across the patrolled range to the east. The door is always barred, though. Other folk live in the warren ruins that someone told him had been a barracks once, but he and Silla keep to themselves.

Arda ignores the sound. He stays at the first room's window to watch the Clearmoon climb a ladder of cloud that streaks the sky. But then again, a murmur. An echo. Whispers held up to a bad mirror, reflected back as pale shadows of themselves. A scowling sound, fingertips on glass, the near-silence of a lost breath.

"Silla?" He speaks to the empty space that spreads around him. "You should rest." He turns reluctantly and looks for her, blinking back the gloom.

In the second room, the candle burns low as Arda approaches quietly, Silla's shape distinct beneath the twisted cloak. She breathes slowly, shallow, still sleeping. He walks the shadow-washed walls to the sealed window, listening. The cold is at the canvas, faint lines of frost tracing out filigree patterns. Silence beyond.

Through the doorway, he hears the whisper of sand on stone. A shifting fall of words in some too-personal language, unknowable. The faintest trace of footfalls.

The light of the brazier is faint where more spell-fire streaks the wall from long ago. As Arda steps past the canvas of the doorway, he thinks he sees a rough outline of black. A shadow like the darkness that comes after staring at the sun. It disappears as he blinks.

When he turns back, Silla has risen from the pallet and is watching him, hand at her stomach and face pale against the darkness. The candle gutters. Shadows push out from the walls and are drawn back once more.

"You should rest," Arda tells her. He moves to the brazier, feeding it once more as a chill threads through him.

When he looks back, Silla is in the doorway. She clutches the canvas.

"It hurts." Her small voice is a child's whisper. Brittle words, an echo from cracked stone. "The seer," she says. "Take me to the seer, to the market. Please."

Arda shakes his head. Silla's footsteps on the cold stone of the floor are nearly silent as she turns back toward the pallet and the darkness beyond.

Arda sits close to the brazier, its heat threading through him. Time passes slowly, drifting listlessly. He isn't sure if he dozes or not when he hears a faint hissing, a gust of cold at his back.

Behind him, the door is open. The bar is raised and set aside, the dark night exposed beyond.

Slowly, Arda rises. He steps within the open door for a moment, feeling the embrace of the frigid night. He walks on lumbering feet to the second room. The pallet is stained from the center where the cloak is gone, drying blood spread like the petals of a dark flower. He looks around the empty chamber twice, carries the dying candle to the corners to make sure Silla is gone.

He checks the cinches on his jack and sets a well-patched cloak to his shoulders. He tightens a too-small wool cap on his head, covering his ears to dull the empty silence of the room. He closes the door firmly behind him as he goes.

As Arda walks, his heavy footsteps sound out. Each step firm, a rhythmic drumming on the ice and stone of the rubble field that surrounds the Fastness like a dark stain. The ruined road is dead grey in the Clearmoon's cloud-torn light, slick black in the shadows.

From the twisting maze of tracks and shattered walls ahead, there comes the sudden call of horses and a clatter of hoofbeats. A fast-moving squad of Ilvanghlira wardens races past Arda, invisible where he hears their approach and presses back to the shadows. The patrols sweep the ruins beyond the Fastness at intervals, seeking those like Arda and Silla brave enough to homestead the surrounding ruins. They find those not as careful as Arda and Silla, not smart enough to stay hidden.

Ahead, Arda sees her. Silla is caught in the moon's-light as she steps out from a hiding place of her own, limping. Her erratic stride is broken at irregular intervals, one hand to her stomach beneath the red-black cloak that wraps her tight. He wants to follow but the Ilvani still within sight force him to stand fast in the shadows until they are gone. They wear black cloaks over mirror-gleaming chainmail, the hooves of their white horses striking a storm of sparks off shattered cobbles. The Ilvanghlira carry no lanterns, their bright eyes seeing all in the moon's-light as they race away, finally disappearing beyond the remains of the Human town that once stood here. Cloud roils in a moon-lit sky but the snow is falling harder, twisting in the wake of the riders' passing.

Arda moves along a rubble track that thrusts up from the ice of the road, but a low wall of blackened stone and a row of shattered columns looms suddenly, cutting him off from Silla. She is hobbling forward, the cloak dragging the ground. She walks with a bird's erratic step, stiff-legged through the rubble. Her feet are bare.

She sees him as she turns.

Arda squints, a quick glimpse caught of fear in Silla's eyes as she moves for the shadows of an adjacent lane. He gauges her direction and sees her route in his mind's eye. She is making for the grey line of rubble that marks off the Fastness to the west.

From somewhere behind, Arda hears our voice again as we follow.

Labored panting, words pulled from the scraping breath of pneumonic lungs. Listening, he can make out a shuffling gait, a cripple's walk along the snow-cold stones.

When he turns, he sees only the rubble-strewn road gleaming back at him. The deadened grass at the edge of the cobbles glitters in the moon-bright haze.

Arda is breathing hard as he reaches the storm-wall. In an irregular circle whose circumference is measured in leagues, a great dam of rubble and dust is torn up from the trenched ground like a living wave, held by arcane force to form a roiling haze five strides deep and twice as high. The storm-wall is the protection of the Fastness, a deadly barrier of shards and grit and hissing wind that will flay the flesh from any who try to pass through it. Within the Fastness and without, the Humans who have fled here and the Ilvanghlira who hunt them speak of the storm-wall as the edge of the last free Human lands. Its gale of stone shards rings a settlement of ten thousand refugees that grows with each passing day.

In their time, each of those refugees slipped through the gate of arched stone that opens up as a single point of safe passage through the storm-wall's fury. Arda knows that the gate is Silla's destination, but he slows in his pursuit of her along an expanse of dead shrubs, frost-streaked where they push up through snow and stone.

The muted face of the storm-wall holds breaks for those who know how to find them. Transient spaces within the deadly haze of debris that can be sensed and timed and used as gates for those brave enough to race through them. This is Arda's purpose, and has been for a space of seasons now, since he and Silla walked to the Fastness from the village where they grew up. Arda's last sight of that home was the black smoke of the burning, and the Ilvani riding a tight circle around the perimeter to herd survivors toward the slave train that takes them north.

Arda was special, his mother always said. She was born to a sorcerous line whose power ran back generations, and she had tried and failed to shape that gift in her son. But even without the ability to direct the power of the arcane to spellcraft, Arda can sense that power in his own blood. He feels its shape and pulse when his mind is clear, and so it is that he watches and waits and steps within the gale of stone and grit that is the storm-wall, stepping into the scant space of one of the fleeting holes that marks its great length.

Even with the power that grants him the storm's sight, the passage through the tempest of thunder and shadow is a dance that promises death at the first unwary step. As always, Arda's senses flag within the dark, within the pounding din of shattered stone, of howling wind. As always, he looks deeper. Looks inside himself, eyes closed as he twists and pulls his way through isolated pockets of empty air. An endless coil of stillness twists ahead of him, the snaking center of a whirlpool turned to its side, embracing him, calling him on. Each step pulls him through to the next, skin rubbed raw with each blast of sand, blood at his ears and nose from the pressure of wind that slams down like a hammer blow.

In the scream of that storm, Arda hears our voice. But then he is gone beyond it. Out through the twisting tunnel of safe passage to the still air beyond.

Within the storm-wall, the Fastness is a sea of light and movement. Arda fights to breathe, staggers with the weight of his exhaustion, the strength drained from him by the surge of arcane power that comes from his mother's blood. He squints against the brightness and the faint sheen of sweat at his eyes, chilled by the frozen air. As far as he can see, shelters and tents and stalls spread like a field of misshapen barrow mounds. A taller framework of stone defines the space of those mounds where ruined walls stand as shroud-line points, ropes and canvas spreading between them like an erratic spider's web. Fires blaze in all directions, but only a scant few of those send smoke skyward. All the rest is arcane flame, unwavering sorcerers' light, and the heat of spellcraft warding off the winter night.

He sniffs cautiously as he slips out of the shadows, the Fastness at night a confusion of sounds and smells and faces that make his head hurt. Things moving. Too many people watching him in the way he doesn't like as he pushes slowly into the clamor and stench of the shelters and the crowd that throngs there.

The Fastness is a Human enclave, home to the descendants of mages and sorcerers, alchemists and artificers. Those who can channel the arcane force in defiance of the will and edict of the hated Ilvani, who hold and breed and work their slaves as beasts. The Ilvani are the Ilvanghlira, the First Folk, fair and deadly and merciless where they swept across the Six Kingdoms of Dugarana six score years past. Ilvani and Human were kin once, or so the half-blood issue of their trysts proves. And so the half-bloods were the first to die, burned down by arcane fire that was sentence of death and funeral pyre all at once.

Arda is taller than most of the figures he passes by a good head-and-a-half, but he stretches even more to keep the distant gate in sight, ranked by a guard force of sullen-eyed battle-casters whose power can lay waste to armies if challenged. The arcanists who founded the Fastness raised the storm-wall with the strength of spellcraft and ancient lore, and the protective shroud has grown in strength all the years since. Arcane might steeps the blood of those who flee here over long years, building an enclave powerful enough that even the Ilvani fear to enter it.

The Ilvanghlira lost the first dozen patrols they sent to test the storm-wall's strength, then pulled back to leave the folk of the Fastness to their doom. Their patrols in the outskirt ruins do little more than slow the influx of escaped slaves for whom the Fastness has quickly become a legend. The last free Human settlement in a land where Human kingdoms dwelled alongside Ilvani holds for five thousand years.

At the gate, Silla limps in from the shadows. Arda watches her slight figure stumble, threading through the drifting crowd. He waits for her to draw closer, not wanting to reveal himself to the gate guards who know his power to sense the weakness in the storm-wall, and who know that he defies the will of the Fastness to trade that power to smugglers and refugees and merchants who have reasons to avoid the gate's scrutiny. The laws of the Fastness dictate that only those possessed of arcane blood are permitted refuge within the storm-wall. But as word spreads of an enclave of free Human folk set at the heart of the endless expanses of the slave camps, the stream and tide of all folk who escape those camps to seek shelter here has ever grown, arcane blood or not.

It is those folk that Arda seeks out within the ruins, or they seek him. For food and fuel and trinkets and coin that he can trade in the Fastness, he leads them through the storm-wall and turns them loose to make their way, and he does not think on what happens to them if they are found out.

The shadows all around him are movement. The faint flicker of following steps, bare foot-sounds on frozen stone. From the corner of Arda's eye, small shapes whisper and shift past and around him, but when he tries to focus on them, they are gone. He slips through a haze of wood smoke and the smell of roast meat, tracking to where he sees Silla moving, but she is gone suddenly in the crowd. Faces to all sides. A chill runs from them to Arda like they can see him without looking. He pushes on, shuts the faces and the voices out.

Then along the line his eye draws out where Silla walks, Arda catches sight of the seer. He pushes his way through the throng to move beyond the tents, then moves faster through the open space of a rough lane. He sees a lean boy in an oversized jerkin packed with rags against the cold, crouched low across an open space of cracked flagstones to sketch a portrait in chalk that gleams with its own arcane light. A face with no eyes, mouth wide in fear or pain. The boy's eyes are green where he looks up to watch Arda pass by.

Beneath the still-standing arch of a fallen wall, the seer sits cross-legged before an Ilvani war-helm turned to a makeshift brazier. Overhead, tattered canvas stretches on twisted wooden poles. Stones and talismans are spread on the ground before her, tokens of feather and bone and crystal. Her hands move where colored tiles of delicate ceramic are laid in formless patterns, spread haphazardly like she and they and the stones and the tent have been dropped here. On the cards are symbols Arda cannot read.

Coal fire and incense trace wisps of black that rise through the cold air as he steps close. The seer hears him, gazing up with an expression of recognition that defies the blindness of milk-white eyes in a scarred face.

"Where is Silla?" Arda says, and his voice is firm. "I saw her come this way."

The seer rocks gently back and forth in a shroud of tattered blanket and thickly layered shawls. "Why do you want her, boy?"

Arda has to fight to listen, her words almost carried away unheard on the drifting wind. "She's lost," he says after a moment. "We must get home."

The seer laughs then. Arda thinks she must not have heard. "We must get home," he says again.

"Silla is home," the seer says.

"Silla is lost. I keep her safe."

The seer smiles, white eyes catching the gleam of red-black coals. "All are lost," she says. "Balance is lost. The dividing line between life and death was lost when the world fell." She passes a hand over the fire, which flares brighter in response, flaring blood-red where she holds a life-shard in her gnarled fingers.

"In the world that was," the seer says in a voice like frosted steel, "balance held." Arda doesn't want to hear her, tries to turn from her voice, but somehow the words fill his mind all the same. "In the world that was, the blood of light pushed through the body of darkness and maintained the life of the whole in steadiness. But now the darkness lives with pulse and breath of its own."

Arda remembers his mother's face suddenly, like he almost never does. He remembers her voice, which is an echo suddenly of the seer's own. Things his mother told him. The old stories.

"In three generations of slavery that the Elf-folk have yoked upon us, they are corrupted by shadow. Evil reshapes the magic of the once-fair, and now that shadow magic builds a barrier between soul and body that spreads in the aftermath of every life lost to the wasting."

Arda's mother was a healer, and she told him of animys and mana, the magic of life and the arcane. But animys and the life it channels are hated by the Ilvani, who seek it out and slay all those who carry it. They shatter the temples of the gods whose divine power bequeaths the life that means nothing to the Ilvani. After the half-bloods, the healers were the next to die.

"For three generations of slavery, the Ilvani that crush the Human populations of the Six Kingdoms have sought out and destroyed the power of animys. The life-magic is waning, all but forgotten. The arcane force reshapes life, the balance shifted."

The seer reaches for him. Arda lurches back, not fast enough. She clutches his hand with fingers whose strength is a raptor's strike, her skin like worn leather. "For all time," she says, "the strength of the living outnumbers the strength of the dead. Until these days. For now the strength of life fades, and the spirits of the dead grow impatient with waiting for the rebirth promised them. Now, the shadow spreads. It sees all. It waits and watches. But spread even so far as it may, there are those who it cannot touch, and you must understand this."

Arda asks for the last time. "Silla."

"She is light," the seer says. "She is one whom the shadow cannot touch. Understand this or be consumed by the shadow that seeks to live in her embrace."

Arda says nothing more as he breaks her grip with a twist of his hand. His fingers are numb suddenly. He squeezes them to a fist to try to force blood to flow.

"The spirits of the dead have no life to return to, and so drink of the power of the arcane that corrupts the force of life and the way of return." The haze of incense twists in with the seer's breath, frozen fast on the air. "The dark spirits now watch over those who channel the light," she whispers.

In the distance, Arda sees Silla watching him. Across a crowd huddling close to the warmth of a spell-fire furnace, one momentary meeting of eyes pulls her out from the anonymous mass, locking Arda to her gaze.

"Their eyes live beyond the darkness, and those eyes watch jealously to see the light despoiled."

Behind him, Arda hears a scuttling laugh. Faint shiftings through the shadow where patched canvas flaps, dark mutterings through closed lips. But when he turns, quicker this time, he sees only the boy still scribbling the blank face in its sightless scream.

When he looks back, the seer's white eyes are closed.

Arda's gaze tracks the blood-stained cloak slipping out toward the haze of stone shadow that marks the rise of the temple ruins in the distance. As he pushes through the crowd that quickly eclipses Silla, he feels the reflex of movement away from him. All around, a wave of unease pulses, figures moving back with hands exposed to threaten the power that lurks there, eyes up as he presses past with the width of his shoulders and the height that lifts him above their heads. Then they are behind him as he hits the open track winding between shelters, and he will not think about them anymore. The dark glaze of his eyes watches Silla stumble as she sees him and starts to run.

Silla holds her own power, but neither of them has ever known what that power is. The arcane force threads her blood as it threads Arda's, enough for her to gain passage at the storm-wall's dark gates where the mages look deep into blood and mind and turn back all who fail their tests. However, not even the mages of the Fastness can tell what gift is Silla's legacy, waiting still for its signs to make themselves clear.

Between the storm-wall and the temple, a broken courtyard stretches silver under new snow where the Clearmoon slips from shredding cloud. The folk of the Fastness keep their shelters away from the temple grounds, showing a kind of reverence for the lost power of that place that Arda does not understand. The shadows of shattered columns, of the statues of the gods, are black on black, spreading from an empty colonnade to rise in the darkness beyond the limit of sight. Across from him, an iron fence stands dark with rust and shadow, even as gravel and dead grass beyond is turned to bright steel by moon's-light and frost.

In that shimmering light, a trail of black spots is spread. Darker than the other blacks of grit and rubble, of grime, of the tracks left by slow-moving feet come here to pray for salvation that has yet to come. Arda bows to the Clearmoon as he stoops, his silhouette stretched out behind him, impossibly tall. The shorter shadows of his hands touch down to come away with a trace of red. He stands, reflexively rubbing them, blood and melting snow churned to sludge between thick fingers.

From somewhere on the courtyard, he hears Silla cry out.

At the shattered temple's edge, a lone tree stands. A single stricken oak in a line of stumps, lost now to long winter and decay. Beyond it there might have been a lawn once. It is darker here, but the Clearmoon's brightness claws out through cloud to touch the uneven ground, shimmering the moss-crusted dark.

Through a break in the iron fence where a gate stood once, Arda sees her propped up on thin arms. Silla is bent low to the ground, an insect shape within the skin of cloak that wraps her. Her hoarse gasp breaks the hiss of rising wind, thinly falling snow swirling to a screen of white. She lifts her head, her face below rough-cut hair turned to jaundiced leather in the shadows. Her lips are charred paper, eyes the color of spoiled milk. Arda sees her chest lower and rise as she leans into the ground's embrace.

A third time, she cries out.

From the nearby dark, Arda hears our voice call in answer.

A guttural throat sound, the growl of an unappeased hunger. The echo of slaughterhouse screams, bile trapped in a choking throat.

He does not look back, moving quickly instead to swing himself across the ruined fence. He lands heavily, sees where Silla tries to run but falls along the broken ground at the lawn's edge. The soil is frost-heaved between ranks of splintered gravestones, Silla stumbling, not seeing. Her legs are splayed, back arched by the gentle curve of the mound of frost and earth beneath her.

Rough scrub willow rises wild along the lawn's edge, branches bare and aloof to the frost whose bite Arda feels through jack and cloak. He reaches Silla to kneel at her side, her face obscured within the haze of white his breath makes. The rough edge of one finger traces a shaking line along her cheek.

"It's cold," he says. Silla shivers as if in answer, one long tremor that starts in the small of her back and spreads. He watches it reach up to touch her lips, climb down to caress her pale feet, the speed of slow waves on still water.

"Come home," he says.

Trembling, Silla shakes her head. Her lips are edged with silver, the color of the frost-deadened grass, trembling as she murmurs words Arda cannot hear. He bends closer.

As her hand comes into view, he sees the shape of shadow in its grip. In the moon's-light, granite flashes dully, Arda turning too slowly, too weary to avoid the shard of stone in Silla's shaking grasp. She hits him hard, just behind the forehead, the soft part of the temple.

He reaches for her as she strikes him a second time. He hears her cry out. A flare of light fills one eye, but he sees the fear in her as he staggers back, falling to the frozen ground like a shattered tree, lightning-struck.

Blinking, breath coming fast, Silla look around her, unsure. Shadow shapes play at the edge of her sight, eyes wide. Tears crystallize, cling to torn lashes and split the image of white and black that looms around her. The bowl of dark sky, the pale streaks where cloud and falling snow scar the Clearmoon's light.

For a moment, silence falls. She pushes herself back, the stone falling from her frozen hand to break the frost-cropped grass.

Then with a gasping shout of pain, Arda rises up suddenly across from her. Blood runs freely from his face. Silla manages to scream, manages to stumble back past his grasp as a shadow-streaked hand shoots out to grab her, thick fingers clutching closed on her ice-cold arm.

From behind, Arda hears a cold stone echo, but he does not look to see.

In Silla's eyes, he sees the pain driven in like nails beneath the hammer of his heavy gaze. Her mouth is tight with fear and pain as she tries to push back along the frost-streaked ground, but Arda's grip is iron. The Clearmoon frames his face, darkening the blood that clouds his eyes.

"You should have come home," he says.

Silla breaks his grip finally with a desperate strength she does not know is in her. Numb, she turns and flees into darkness. Brushing the fence with a thin shoulder, she pulls herself through the ruined gate. Behind her, Arda vaults the iron, landing heavily. His footsteps are faster than hers, pounding after her, steady. He grabs her as she runs, Silla stumbling, spilling to the ground.

"Come home," he says. "I don't want to hurt you. Just stop."

"Stay away." Silla's voice is glass, words pushing past cold lips, a swollen tongue, her throat rubbed raw suddenly.

From ahead, from the dark space where the ruined courtyard opens up, Silla hears our voice whisper an answer. Unknown words thread through slow footfalls. An echo of Arda moving behind her, except he has already stopped. Staring around him suddenly.

Faltering, Silla crawls ahead. Lost in shadows, waiting for some sympathetic hand from the darkness.

Arda's foot catches her between the shoulders instead, one boot pushing hard where the rubble rises up to meet her. She feels the warmth of blood at her nose, on her hands where she tries to rise. She has no breath to cry out as he leans close over her, no face except the shadow that scours the ground where the Clearmoon embraces him.

"You should have come home."

In answer, Silla hears a dark intake of breath. An echo of anguish, a quiet sound of tears that knows no respite from ever-unseen pain.

She tries to blink. Tries to see into the shadow where the erratic motion of snow drifts through islands of isolated moon's-light.

She hears a whispered word of solace. She hears the report of lonely laughter trapped between narrow walls. In the darkness, something scratches the crust of frozen ground, touches the shadows with a tongue, tastes the earth and air. The rasping of breath through eager teeth, the gaze of ever-open eyes.

"Please," Silla whispers, but Arda answers her with a slow movement that brings him down to kneel at her back. His hands are cold at her neck as he squeezes.

In the darkness, frost and darkness frame a whisper of hate. Behind her, in front. Circling wider, an erratic staccato of footfalls carry out across the numbed and silent earth.

Something watches her as she watches back. Silla hears a whisper of peace as a sudden darkness cloaks her.

When she opens her eyes again, she is kneeling four strides away from where Arda lies. Around him, the snow runs red-black, thick shadow-trails that follow the contours of frost and earth, blurring out to darkness in the dying grass.

The storm-wall courses past her, shifted suddenly from its course along the edge of the Fastness, and its muted pulse of wind and rending stone is muted further by our voice as it slips within her, warms her with its touch.

She hears screams from the light beyond the temple, from the shelters and stalls and tents, that tell her this is not a dream.

The raging wall of rubble and grit is moving, bending toward her. Its roiling face melts the falling snow to a slick screen of water that hangs like a shield of glass, shimmering as it gently washes the blood from her hands, thin rivulets flowing away to the air.

The storm of shards and dust has slain Arda, flensing cloak and jack, flesh and muscle to bloody strips. He is long and thin and bright against the white of the frost-touched ruins and the moon's-light that catches faint flecks of red along the courtyard stones. He is pinned to the earth with spikes rendered of rib and shattered bone, driven down through stomach and limbs, through the remains of the throat beneath the slack apprehension of his face.

Silla stares at that face for a long while. Then she looks away.

From the shadows beyond the dead oak, we speak to her, unseen. A rough-edged shape, shuffling on soft claws in the dark. A scent of lost things and the sullen pain of eyes that never blink. Silla shivers, a deep convulsion of the emptiness inside her, of the breath of life that will not come.

In the intermittent light, behind the mask of falling snow, she feels the crouching shape that her eye tries and fails to hold. A shifting field of black flecks. Our voice that her ear senses but does not recognize. Not yet. Throat-bound tongues, an empty echo.

From the edge of the courtyard come the words that speak of shivering in winter's embrace, alone. The echo of things said when no one is listening. A child's cry. The sound of lives spent in patient waiting.

From behind her, Silla hears the tick of feet on frozen stone, gravel on gravel. She hears the sound of breathing, the black mouth of solitude, the quick rasp of fear that she understands suddenly is not hers alone.

And as she breaks the silence with dark laughter, she feels the joy of something yearning to life as it brushes her hand, kissing her with the warmth of budding lips. She hears the voices of the dead that circle her, whose lives are magic and shadow and who have woven themselves into the arcane storm that protects the Fastness. The life-magic waning, the arcane force reshaping it to protect the last free Humans in Dugarana.

Silla feels the connection that binds her to the shadow and its voice, twisting through the emptiness in her belly and heart.

She stands slowly and wraps her arms around herself, lifting her head to the dark as she feels the strengthening rise and fall of her chest. The pulse of blood at her throat, at her chest is slowing. Her ears catch at our voice all around her, picking at words she can feel but not hear.

She is home.

A sound of joy and sadness escapes her, caught on the rising wind.

— A **Space** Between —

THEY WERE FOUND in the midst of their tryst by the Khanan Irnash'an himself, the steel-bound door of the abandoned White Tower gallery breaking beneath his shoulder like it might have been a courtesan's cork-paneled closet. The voice of the High Emperor of all Ajaeltha when he saw them was a scream of purest rage. He held the scepter of his reign in hand, hefted like a mace with all the strength and fury that had conquered the uprisings of three governors before the two of them were even born.

Jalina screamed, clutching the sweat-stained satin sheet to her as she scrambled back on the cushioned pallet, eyes downcast from instinctive deference as much as fear. Charan met the aging sovereign's gaze as the scepter swung high. He hit the floor rolling, naked flesh slamming against cold stone as the mass of gilt-edged steel and razor-sharp gems hissed past his head, a finger's breadth from killing him.

Across the ancient line of statues set in an uneven colonnade to both sides of the door, his clothing was scattered as an unseemly web. Cloak and leggings, shirt and linens. The stone faces were ancient courtiers and forgotten sovereigns, all of them staring blankly. Banished here to dust and silence, far from the white marble of the khanan's great halls.

Jalina would be safe enough, Charan knew as he scrambled to his feet, feeling the ancient warrior twisting behind him but not daring to look. He understood that the second blow would come for him, just as he knew that it would hit with certainty, no room to maneuver in the narrow confines of the cluttered chamber. Snatching at his leggings and belt, Charan grabbed up his knife, the scabbard left exposed as it always was. Force of habit. He spun as he hurled it with no thought, felt the momentum of his movement twist through his arm like the crack of a teamster's whip.

He was planning only to distract the khanan, hoping to divert that follow-up killing stroke to his shoulder or side rather than his skull. What he might do to prevent the next blow was a matter he was still frantically thinking on when the scepter lurched from callused hands.

The khanan clutched at the knife where a hand's-length of damask steel had buried itself hilt-deep in his chest. He hit the floor with a soft thud and the gasp of his last breath. All was silent after that.

Neither of them spoke for a long while. Charan fought to slow his breathing, realized numbly that the continued quiet meant the khanan had made his careful way up the tower stairs alone. He slipped to the buckled door, closed it carefully against its shattered frame.

"You killed him," Jalina whispered at last. The ash-brown eyes were wide, set within their frame of auburn hair. Her hands were shaking, fingers reflexively forming the deathsign before her.

"A knife in the heart will do that."

Charan stood over the corpse, turned from her so she wouldn't see the wonder as he stared. It wasn't the first body he had seen. Not even the first whose death was nominally his responsibility, but it was the first to have fallen by his own hand. He half-expected to feel something. Fear, perhaps. The weight of hubris, the dread of vague doom. Some guilt or misgiving.

Instead, his mind was empty. As he looked down absently, he saw his sex still standing rigid, unhooded where it reached for the empty air before him. He tasted metal in his mouth, dull copper like the stippled blood rising in the khanan's dead eyes.

"He is the khanan and your father," Jalina whispered, hoarse. "Is that all you have to say?"

Charan smiled bitterly. A hand absently ran through the black hair shrouding his face, pushed it back to hang to his shoulders. He turned to his sister with a flash of black eyes that were reflected in her own cold gaze.

"Gods save the empress," he said.

He saw Jalina flush, a rush of crimson rage that made her eyes flash brighter. It twisted from face to neck, pushed down to spread across her breasts as she stood regally, wrapping the sheet around herself.

"We bring him back," she said.

"He's dead," Charan responded idly. "There's a degree of permanence involved."

"I mean bring him to the priests, fool. Impose the rites of return while the spirit still lingers…"

"When the spirit returns, the memory comes with it. Bring him back to recall how I put a blade in his heart? I think not." Charan stooped to lift the diadem from his father's brow, felt the flesh already cooling beneath it. He pulled his shirt from a statue of the great-grandfather who named the empire that his sister had just inherited, dropped it to shroud the face and its sightless eyes.

There was less blood around the knife than he imagined there would be. He absently tossed the crown over his shoulder, turned to see Jalina snatch it by instinct before it hit her. By a less well-practiced instinct, she recoiled from it like it might have been a serpent, sending it to the ground with the dull thud of its golden weight.

"I thought you might like to try it on," Charan said evenly.

"It fits your ambition best." His sister's voice was ice, the full mouth set in an imposing blank line.

He only shrugged. "Should have thought on that before you clawed your way from mother's womb ahead of me."

He saw her look away, close her eyes and mark the deathsign again in response to the mention of their mother. The maker's cross, both hands scribing the air before her. The circle of the sun above, the quick intersection of the sword below.

Charan scowled. "No matter how often you wave your hands to your gods, she stays just as dead."

Jalina dropped the sheet as she stood, slunk to the window ledge where she carefully folded her own clothing. She stood in silence a while. "I want neither the crown nor the throne," she said at last. "I'll refuse both. Take them and be happy for the first time in your life."

Charan's dark eye followed the curve of her back as she fastened her underskirts, the faint gleam of lantern light showing the wetness at her thighs and in the dark tangle of her sex. He felt the ache in his loins thicken.

"Our first purpose here will make us both happier by far," he said carefully. "For a time, at least."

He saw the shudder of revulsion slip through his sister. As from a sudden shock of cold water, his tumescence waned.

"You stopped needing to prove your depravity to me long ago." Jalina's hair showed whorls of sun-brightened copper in the light as she tied it back, tightened a belt of spun sheen-silver to fasten her shift. This she adjusted to the courtly style, the globes of her breasts revealed from the wide-cut sleeves.

"My so-called depravity has had no shortness of call from you these past years." But his sister was silent as she slipped her knife in its scabbard to her thigh, adjusted a patterned skirt of blue and yellow silk over it.

Charan turned from her in anger, tripped over something. At his feet, their father's body. He stared at it like it a thing suddenly and somehow forgotten.

"We need to think," he said.

"Match our stories up." Jalina's voice was a child's suddenly. Charan heard it as he dressed with his back to her, saw a vision of her in his mind suddenly at age twelve, their mother dead that summer. In her chamber in the White Tower of the Empress, in the scant time before the priests arrived and the body was whisked away, both he and his sister had seen the marks of his father's hands at her throat.

When the spirit returns, the memory comes with it.

Charan remembered the brown eyes wet with tears, his sister's hand in his as the sepulcher stones were sealed in a haze of blue-white fire. An eldritch consumption, the healers called it. Beyond their skill to pull her back from the darkness. The people had believed them, because it was easier that way.

"We can say we found him," Jalina whispered. "Throw a concubine or two to the councilors. A crime of passion."

"No."

"Assassination, then. Lure a guard here, make it look as though…"

"No," Charan said carefully. "No story. Anything we do, any involvement with the body, no matter how fleeting, makes us suspect."

"Then what…"

"We dispose of it."

In the sigh that followed a sullen silence, Charan knew that Jalina had already realized there was no other way forward. She needed Charan to be the first to voice it, though. As always, he thought.

"A place no one will ever go." He prodded the body with his foot, felt it unyielding but with no stiffness of the blood yet. The last of his own stiffness had finally faded.

"They won't believe we know nothing of this."

"They will when we show our surprise. Show our uncertainty along with everyone else at the khanan's disappearance…"

"You're as big a fool as he was. The councilors will look to us…"

"They won't dare. The hint of murder puts the empire in their hands, yes. But an unexplained disappearance creates a constitutional crisis that threatens the council's hold on power. Let them come up with the idea of covering for it. They'll invite the two of us to rule as regents in father's place. Tell the people he's gone in secret to the temples at Terhetu, or leading a warband to the Dragonspires."

He looked back quickly, saw her force the quiet smile from her lips. Her eyes were ice where she watched him. Dry, suddenly. He hadn't seen her wipe the tears away.

"What do we do?" she said.

The castle was dark, the corridor lanterns shrouded, but the light of the near-full Clearmoon at the windows was a bright guide as they made their way slowly from the White Tower, down to the distant kitchens far below. The first leg down the endless winding stairs was the hardest, both of them staggering. They had stripped the body, using the robes to staunch the slow flow of blood. Then they wrapped their father in the silk sheets, Charan taking him by the shoulders, descending backwards to watch Jalina struggle as she gripped his feet and followed. The scepter, Charan had lashed tight to his father's waist with the jeweled belt he wore, its bone-crushing weight a scarcely noticed addition to their father's well-muscled bulk.

They moved in a regular pattern, setting the corpse down so that Charan could scout ahead, listening with held breath and pulsing heart for the telltale sound of footsteps. It was late enough that there was little chance of them being seen in the side corridors and wall-passages they moved along, but he had no great desire to explain his presence. Or, more inevitably, to make more murder against whatever courier or wayward servant they happened across.

As disturbing as that thought was, he knew with unasked certainty that he would do the deed without hesitation if it came to it. One death on his hands and he was still shaking. He would have expected that to make the next harder.

Through the wide-open windows, the heat of day was finally past, broken by the dark breeze of the bay. Moon's-light gleamed silver on the water, gold on the towers and minarets of Sasaerin, jewel of Ajaeltha. The city's sloping peaks of clustered spires rose across from them as he and Jalina descended, working from the castle's upper tiers to the servants' levels below.

Luck or fate was on their side, it seemed. Charan could hear slaves in the kitchen along the final stretch of darkened corridor, but the cutting room adjacent was empty. He caught the familiar steel tang of sanguine air as he thrust open the damp-swollen door, saw a half-dozen yearling buffalo dressed and hanging in the darkness. He was much younger the last time he had any reason to pass this way, but a quick inspection showed that the wide black grate at the center of the stained stone floor still hadn't been repaired in all the time since.

When they had dragged their father's body inside, Charan pushed the door shut, kicked a wedge of splintered bone from the detritus of the floor into place along its foot to jam it. He leaned across a dark-stained table, needed to rest his aching back a moment. Across from him, Jalina limped as she paced, staring around her.

"You're a fool," she said at last, as he knew she would.

"I'll take that under advisement."

"You think they won't search for him here? Or were you planning to cut and dress him for feast and hope no one notices?"

Charan moved past her to drop to his knees. He gripped the stinking grate, ignored the heady slime of blood and offal that clung to its corroded bars as he shifted it from practiced memory. A particular twist, a specific positioning that would disengage it from the stones that surrounded them. He felt it come loose, lifted it carefully. Below, the mouth of a narrow well opened up to darkness.

The khanan's stiffening legs were forced into that darkness only with effort, but Charan needed to use the steel and gold scepter to shatter the bones of his father's splayed arms and wide-set shoulders. A half-dozen blows forced the torso into the space of the drain, the broken arms up in a dark gesture of surrender as Charan pushed down with his foot. He kicked a half-dozen times to force the mangled corpse through, watching as it slipped away finally with a sickening lurch.

He dropped the scepter after it, heard the faint echo a moment later as both it and the body hit water below.

"The sewers?" Jalina said from behind. "They'll search every sewer and tunnel within a league of the castle to find him."

"If you insist on telling me things I already know, put them to a tune, at least." With a flourish, Charan stood back, beckoning her toward the open sluice drain. The day's wash water was still slick on the stones, dripping at the edges like a rank rain.

"You're mad," she said.

"And a fool, apparently, and proud of both. Get in."

"I will not..."

"You will," Charan said, "whether you climb or whether I drop you." Smiling, he advanced on his sister as one moved on a disobedient dog, saw her flinch despite her own best effort. "This isn't done yet, but when it is, you'll have an empire to rule. The scent of blood is the first thing you need to get used to."

He held her ashen gaze, felt the depth of the anger there. Anger and something else, but he had no time to try to read it.

Not fear, he knew. Of all his sister's moods, that alone was the one he would always recognize.

Jalina turned away. She stepped to the mouth of the black well.

"There's a ladder," Charan said, more softly. "The smell is worse above. Hold your breath to the bottom, you'll be fine."

The narrow chute was roughly chiseled, a wide drain descending what might have been the length of two dozen paces. As his sister lowered herself, Charan saw her find the ladder, its rungs inexplicably extending a hand's-breadth from ancient stone with no sign of support. Steel cylinders descended the length of the shaft, thin as a finger and impossibly strong, hung there and protected from corrosion by the unseen strength of spellcraft. He had stolen them from his father's arcane armories on a whim when he was a boy, even before he had any idea what use he might eventually put them to.

She needed both hands to cling carefully as she descended. Charan went one-handed, the other holding an evenlamp he had taken from the corridor along the way, its eternal cold flame casting the glow of an unnatural sunrise across the stones. He slid the grate back into place from below as he made his way down.

The air was cloyingly damp, Charan's light shimmering on water below them. He heard Jalina jump to wet stone as she reached the bottom, her footsteps loud but steady. He was behind her a moment later. Their father's shrouded body lay in a shallow puddle of black water. Charan stepped over it carefully.

The ceiling was barely tall enough for him to stand beneath, vaulted stone holding the weight of ground and castle above, slick with moisture and the sheen of black mold. True to his word, the air within the sewer passage was clean, scoured by the salt tang of the sea. The broad tunnel was of finished stone but had no entrance, no exit, no doors. The well they had just descended opened up as a rough chute in the arched ceiling. Midway along the walls, a dozen vents opened up to darkness, each as wide across as a child's shoulders.

On the wall beneath the ladderway, a larger grate opened up, as wide to the eye as the drain in the cutting room above. Charan stepped close to it, Jalina staring, her expression unreadable.

"You've been here before?"

Charan ignored her. "Look here," he said instead.

The bars of the slime-slick grate were set at cross-angles a hand's-width apart. Beyond them, a shadowed tunnel of cracked and blackened brick opened up, a grated aqueduct whose mouth dripped water in an intermittent rhythm. A distant pulsing roar echoed from the darkness.

"It connects to the harbor, beyond the deep docks," Charan said. "Seawater flows in at high tide to clean out this and all the other sewer traps beneath the castle. As the tide turns, it empties again. We remove the grate. We ensure the body can't be identified." He felt his hand absently stray to his knife, forced it away. "Let the sea take what we leave of him. Consign him to the depths."

The grate was black sea-iron, strong as crucible steel but untouched by rust. The stones around it were weaker, however, their mortar eaten away by age and the salt-rot of the sea. Charan pulled a chunk free with little effort, tossed it to the black water where his father's body lay.

"Tear a stone wall down with our bare hands?" In Jalina's voice, he heard a familiar disdain that told him she had secretly appraised and approved of the plan. "We'll be here a week," she said. "They'll be looking for him and us before we're halfway finished."

Charan smiled as he suddenly grabbed for the wall, pulled himself up as the jet of water he had heard approaching broke through the bars. He watched it crash across their father, breaking along the stone floor to make Jalina scramble back. It pooled in a slick haze, ankle deep now. The inflow returned to a trickle, steady against the distant howl of the surf.

Charan set the evenlamp on an outcropping near the ceiling. "Then we'll need to work more quickly than that," he said.

They labored together wordlessly, side by side in the wet gloom, knives hacking at the crumbling mortar that held twisted bars to weathered stone. At intervals, Charan struck the grate hard with his father's scepter, gold plating and gems worth a rogue's fortune torn away with each echoing blow. Jalina glanced above her each time he hit, but he knew from experience that no sound would make its way up the dark well to the castle above.

His shoulders were already aching, but he wouldn't let Jalina see it. He watched her as he worked because she was refusing to meet his gaze, focused wholly on the digging. She paused only when one end of her knife's guard snapped off at her attempt to use it as a lever. The deathsign she made at regular intervals didn't slow her down. One hand working, the other with fingers twisting to ward off the fear that he knew her father's body was inspiring in her. She would whisper names each time, a faint trace of movement at her pale lips. Benedictions and the names of deities long dead.

"The gods have already had their say in the matter of the khanan's life," Charan said quietly. "What do you hope they add to it now?"

Jalina's eyes narrowed as she redoubled her attack against the ruined wall. "Mock my faith all you wish."

"I don't mock your faith. I'm thinking I should embrace it. Seek the guidance of sun and moons as did the khanans of old." He twisted his knife, feeling for and carefully avoiding its breaking point as he dug his way into crumbling stone.

The fear had been in Jalina when their mother died. Charan felt it that day when her hand found his at the edge of the funeral bier. He felt it that night when he drew her to him for the first time, yielding when he pressed his mouth to hers. He felt it as he led her through silence and shadow up to the White Tower that had been their mother's court, empty since the week of mourning, its servants feted and drugged and burned still living with their empress-consort on the pyre.

"The khanans of old Ajelast were masters of sun and moons." Jalina took the bait, as he knew she would. "The god-emperors captured the magics of the heavens, and with it built a world the likes of which will never be seen again."

Twenty centuries before, Ajelast had been built on the bones of the great empire of Nesana that died out in fits of corruption and bloody magical war long ago in its homeland across the sea. In an age where the secrets of magic were long divided between the power of life and the power of mana, the animys and the arcane, it was the hierophants of Nesana who had married and perfected those disparate sorceries, and who were the power behind the ancient empire of Eria that first bound the lands of the western Leagin as one.

"Your precious Empire cast down that faith and made all Ajaeltha slaves to others' ambition," Jalina said, defiant. "Even as they stole the power that was once ours. Those who revere the Lothelecan are the dogs never knowing any life but the search for scraps at their masters' feet."

With one final thrust, the last mortar holding in the left side of the grate fell away beneath his knife. His father's blood still clung to the grooves of the blade, he saw.

"The khanans of old Ajelast married blood to blood," he said. "Brother to sister."

Charan watched a darkness fall across Jalina's face like a mask. She turned all her attention to the keystone at the upper corner of the grate that had loosened but would not yet move. He stepped in behind her, slipped his hand in to grasp it. She flinched as he pressed against her.

"It is not for anyone else to tell us what we can and cannot do. Not anymore." Charan's voice was a faint echo over the shadowed rasp of stone on stone. "I do not claim to know the will of heavens or earth or what gods live above or below our own lives. I only know what I believe in, and what I believe in is you."

"It's over, Charan."

There was a resounding crack as the crumbling keystone came loose, a shower of dust and mortar rubble following it. The slow flow of water was disrupted for a moment as the grate lurched. Charan was suddenly very cold.

Jalina threaded herself through his arms and away while he stood unmoving. He watched the stone fall absently from his hand to strike black water.

"We walk this path together," he said, but his voice trailed off against the dripping hiss of the shattered duct. He fought to speak, but his sister's words filled his mind and drove all else out.

He had expected those words, but not here. Had known from the first that this moment would come one day. Jalina pushed along the wall as splashing footsteps, turned back toward him. The brown eyes burned with contempt. The taste of metal came to his mouth again.

"We walk together," he said. "Now more than ever. We pledged oaths…"

"We were children then," Jalina said, and Charan once more heard the child she had been thread through the words. An echo in her voice that cut him. "Children's oaths mean nothing. Set the past behind you, brother."

"We are bound," he said. He sheathed his dulled knife to seize the bars, pulled with all the strength his rising anger gave him so that he wouldn't have to look at her. He heard stone and brick give way, felt the muscles knot across his back and shoulders as the bent and ruined grate shifted in his grasp. "Now more than ever. We…"

"There is no we. Not anymore."

With a rumbling echo of steel and stone, the grate came loose, and the response Charan would have made to his sister was choked off behind that sound and the certainty he heard in her. An argument, he would have expected, could have dealt with. A carefully crafted distraction, his sister jockeying as she so often did for any subtle advantage in the eternal tension that hung between them.

She had sensed the fear in him. Seeing deeper into him, perhaps, than even he was capable of. Using that fear just as he should have expected she would.

He dropped the grate to the pool of the floor, heard its drowned echo ring out.

"Father only just cold, and already you speak with his voice," he said evenly. "He has no say in what we do anymore..."

"What we did," she said, all stress on the past. "What we did, what we were, is why he died."

He felt it then. Saw it like a mirror held up to his own uncertainty. She was testing him, he realized. The fear he had learned to recognize twisted through her words, hiding a truth he could almost see. A thing he could extract and claim if he was careful, as he had been so many times before.

The evenlamp on its shelf shed its light behind him. He moved slowly, Jalina wrapped within his shadow. A hand on her shoulder made her flinch. Then slipping across, rising to her cheek.

"If your gods do exist, it was their hand that guided my blade today. They have brought you here. Placed you at the apex of the power that was promised you the day you were born. They have made you their agent in Ajaeltha now, and placed me here at your side."

Charan didn't see the arch of the ceiling shudder and split above his head until he felt Jalina's hands on his arm.

With a strength he never suspected in her, his sister pulled him off his feet, dragging him backward land atop her across the floor as the age-weakened vault collapsed on the spot where he had been standing. The noise was an echoing roar in the narrow confines of the sewer's stone walls, a blast of stale air slamming past to blind him with grit and black mold.

When he could open his eyes, the chamber was silent once more. The evenlamp had fallen when Jalina saved him, its light shimmering now where it was half-submerged in the ebb and flow of black water. The scepter and the grate were both gone, buried beneath a jumbled fall of shattered brick and rubble rising knee high. A pall of ash-grey dust hung over it, twisting like storm clouds in the uneven gloom.

"My thanks," Charan said awkwardly. He felt his sister push him away as he stood.

Jalina moved back to crouch against the wall, eyes closed and breathing hard. He stepped toward her, touched her shoulder. She didn't flinch this time, but when he put his hand to her waist, she shrugged him off, turned so she could slip past him.

Charan saw the ashen eyes widen, flicking past his gaze to something behind him. The fear he recognized again. He crouched low as he spun by instinct, knife in hand.

At the corner of the haphazard mound of rubble, half-buried and barely visible beneath the fall of stones and shattered brick, a body sprawled.

Charan scooped up the evenlamp, brought it to bear on the apex of the collapsed wall. Through a shattered fissure, he saw darkness opening up above the narrow confines of the sewer chamber. A rising passageway of worked stone, closed off from the trap at some point in the past. Or perhaps an ancient sublevel, beneath which the sewers had been extended when the foundations of the castle were first laid.

"Who is it?"

Jalina was at his side, her fingers trembling as they made the deathsign. Despite himself, Charan fought the hope that those fingers would seek his when they were done, watching as his sister's hand went to her breast instead, clenched tightly there.

The mummified form was the black of weathered silver, wrapped in a torn shroud of rotted cloak and twisted ropes of cobweb. "Dead," Charan answered.

"I can see what it is. I asked who."

"Death makes all the answers the same."

It wasn't the sight of death that his sister feared, Charan knew. It was the spirits of the past. The superstitions of children and old men were the foundations on which the faith of her once-dead gods was built. Their church had been resurrected a generation before in the aftermath of the distant Empire's fall, and while he heard the liturgy as often and as endlessly as she, it had never amounted to any more than any other folk tale in his mind. He had thought his sister of the same mind, once.

When their mother died, Jalina had changed.

"Imperial Ajelasti," Charan said softly as he bent close to the body. Jalina gave him a quizzical look. "Judging by the age of him."

Ajelast, whose ancient empire was the foundation on which Ajaeltha was raised, had been the most bitterly contended of the lands destined to become the Elder Kingdoms. Long after Nesana was only a memory, Ajelast stayed strong. First of the Elder Kingdoms to fight the encroach of Empire. Last to fall to the Lothelecan's iron embrace, or so the official histories said. More accurate accounts told less flattering tales of the complicity of Ajelast's last free khanans in the Empire's final assault against the independence of the east.

However, all tales spoke consistently in describing how Ajelast rose in the aftermath of the fall of Empire as Ajaeltha. A new empire forged in blood and steel by their father's grandfather. A strength for rule in their line that Charan saw in his sister in each waking moment, but which for some reason he had never warmed to himself.

Even under the rule of the Lothelecan, the Ajelasti made sport of assassination like no people before or since. Military history had been Charan's single point of interest in his lessons as a child, forgoing languages, astronomy, natural history, literature and all else in favor of the endless recitation of organized bloodshed that his father's military advisors held in seemingly endless supply. Wars they themselves had seen, political uprisings before their time, endlessly talked of and analyzed. Tales of generals and the nobles who ruled them murdered in more glorious and disturbing ways than Charan would have thought possible.

His father had always spoken proudly of his son's predilection for the bloody politics of history. He found himself wondering now if the khanan's opinion had changed in the last few moments of his life.

Their father's spirit was still locked within his already rotting flesh. Or so it was reckoned by the beliefs of the temple, and by the magic of the priests that could have enervated that dead flesh to life with the ancient rites. For people such as his sister, those rites proved the renewed presence of the once-dead gods. Banished by Empire and lost to the faithless but never truly gone, the priests said. For Charan, however, the rites did the opposite, and he was always quick to point out that the priests' magic functioned just as well under the Empire's godless ochlocracy as it did now.

"Captain or castellan," Charan said idly. "Or a queen's consort, or a king's lover. Killed and sealed up behind stone. Or sealed alive, more likely. Open up the old tunnels beneath any castle, you'll find more like him."

Charan saw his sister make the deathsign again. He let her hear him laugh.

"You spend your life afraid of shadows, you soon fear the sun and moons that shed them."

"I make the mortal warding for you," she said calmly. "Not for me."

Charan felt a flush of heat rise at his chest, twisting up to his cheeks. In his sister's voice, there was a sudden edge that he had heard before and learned to fear. Something had changed in the two dozen words that just passed between them, and he had no idea what it was.

"Do I look afraid, sister?"

"The dead cast their shadows even in the absence of light," Jalina said, not answering. Her face was pale in the glow of the evenlamp, not meeting Charan's dark gaze. The water at the ruined duct was a steady rain now, dripping in an uneven curtain against the stones. "He's been here all along, turning this place to a tomb. You let the dead witness your corruption, their spirit becomes a part of that corruption, tainting it further. Tainting you. You should be afraid."

He understood then. He cursed himself silently, even as he angrily conceded Jalina credit for this thing she had hidden, blindsiding him expertly. His focus on getting their father through the castle, down into his makeshift sewer tomb kept his thoughts scattered. He should have seen it. Would have seen it under any other circumstances.

He laughed in an attempt to cover for the slip, knew that it was already too late. "So my soul is tainted, is it?"

"Brother, your soul was tainted from the moment of your birth."

At the grate above, Jalina had told him she wouldn't descend, her revulsion all too real. But she hadn't bothered asking about their dark destination. Hadn't needed to, Charan realized now, because she already knew where they were going.

"Your darkness brought you to this place from the time you were nine years old," she said simply. "It made you bring a long line of serving girls with you, each discarded with silver in hand when you were done with them. When they had finished pretending they were me."

The words carried themselves with an ease that made Charan knew she had waited years to speak them. He only smiled in return, tried desperately to judge her true tone, her mood. Something was happening. A plan whose foundations were laid long ago. Disrupted now by the death of their father, he guessed. Put into motion early. Or was the khanan's death merely the catalyst? A moment of disaster long waited for, in whose aftermath Jalina would act?

He went for the feint by instinct, summoned up a suitable degree of chagrin that he could pretend was a response to her discovering his secret.

"If only I had known all those years how much the pretending would pale against the reality of you." He stepped close, the sound of his breathing loud even over the hiss of water as Jalina watched. A shiver threaded through her. He moved his head down to kiss the nape of her neck beneath the tightly drawn auburn hair.

He felt her push back against him, too quickly. He lost track of what happened next.

Steel flashed as she spun away from him, his own knife in his hand somehow. They locked guards at the first strike, then Jalina was fading back, footsteps splashing clumsily as her blade slashed past Charan's neck. He slid to let it miss him, parried the next blow, returned with one of his own that she caught and twisted past, behind him suddenly.

Where Jalina crouched, her eyes were bright with the fear he recognized.

"I knew it would end this way," she whispered.

Charan's hand was shaking, the battered blade of his knife weaving points of bright fire in the half-light. He tried to trace back the two dozen heartbeats just past, but his sight, his mind and memory were the same blur of red.

He had drawn on her, he thought. But he wouldn't have. Couldn't have. The evenlamp was in the water behind him. He had dropped it in expectation, needing to free his other hand for balance. Impossible. He shook his head, saw his sister flinch in expectation of another strike.

The feeling he was forever afraid to name rooted deep in his chest. He felt the scent and the sight of her overwhelm his memory.

He felt the pain that her words made, felt the fear in her that was the knowledge that her brother had tried to kill her rather than lose her. The knowledge that he would try again. He felt the weight of the knife in his hand.

At the conduit they had torn free of ceiling and wall, a surge of black water exploded as shadow and white foam. The sea-channel had tipped past the aqueduct's unseen halfway point and was flowing steady now, pressing in with a steady hiss of salt air and the distant moaning of the pounding surf beyond the harbor's breakwater stones.

Charan felt for the hot shard of anger at his breast, cooled it with slow breathing. He lowered his knife as much as he dared without compromising his ability to parry, wasn't sure the notched and blunted blade could even withstand the force of an attack.

"You are the one they will watch," he called, voice as clear as he could make it. "Jalina, whose beauty and grace will redefine an empire in mourning. While all the while, I will be your right hand, silent and invisible and devoted to your bidding. It was fate that brought you first from mother's womb, because you are the one who can lead. Some of us are fated to follow."

Jalina tried to laugh, voice ringing out like a cascade of silver over the dank echo of water on stone. With sudden dread, Charan realized why. He cursed himself for the slowness of his wit. His father's murder had rattled him. His father's death. He corrected himself absently, felt the weight of it press down on him all the same.

"You've spoken those words before," his sister said.

Charan felt the memory of the White Tower twist through him, hot wires beneath his skin. He shook his head but kept his silence.

"Do you think often on that night?" she whispered. "Does the memory come unbidden? And knowing now that it ends, do you feel sorry for yourself, brother?" Her voice was twisted through with a honeyed sweetness that brought the taste of bile to his throat. "Cut off from your carnal sanctuary? Denied this forbidden tryst?"

"It was more than that," Charan said, and he felt his tongue suddenly turn to lead even as the words were formed.

"Whatever you thought it was, Charan, you were wrong."

She struck with the speed of a brush-viper, too fast to see. Charan managed to twist away in the barest nick of time, felt her knife's broken guard tear his tunic and the flesh beneath. And in the sudden blossom of that pain, his only thought was that he would never know whether her renewed fury was a sign that she believed his words. Or the final proof that she didn't.

The flash of blades between them was a steel-grey rain as they fought across the shadows of the rapidly flooding chamber. All the effort and eager practice of two childhoods lost to the training floor of their father's war-masters showed now in the grim set of Charan's mouth, in the smoldering light of his sister's eyes. They hit fast, unforgiving, a succession of killing strokes turned wide by the narrowest of margins. Both their blades dulled by stone but hitting hard enough to punch through skin and bone if they hit, Charan knew. Brother and sister striking like the twin serpents they truly were.

Charan had no illusion about having the speed that would be necessary to disarm his sister, just as he was sure she harbored no vain hope that she might wear him down. A terrible passion twisted between them now that replaced the stolen emotion of the time just passed, of the months before, of the five breathless years since they had first taken each other in the silent aftermath of their mother's ash-rites.

All their lives, mother and father had been the twin poles around which so much turned. With their mother's death, they had found a measure of peace within each other.

With their father's death, they had found something else, it seemed.

But even as he thought it, Charan fought to recognize this rage, this sudden and inescapable fury that twisted between them now with each pass of the blade. A new emptiness, he thought. A space between them that he had never felt before. But in feeling it now, he wondered whether it was a thing that had always been there, hidden by choice and the sweet darkness that cloaked them both, night after long night.

He was breathing hard, heard the roaring in his ears that was more than just the pounding of his blood. His feet were numb, water calf-deep now where the inflow churned it to black foam.

For all the late-childhood trysts that brought him here, Charan had never lingered belowground to watch the high tide cleanse the trap and the sewer channels beyond. He had no idea how long it would take for the water to fill the chamber, but he could guess that the end was coming quickly.

Jalina glanced to one side, avoiding the worst of the spray. Time enough for Charan to move. He drove hard for her heart, couldn't risk pulling the punch of the killing stroke, but even still, he caught her knife instead as it flashed up to parry, impossibly fast. He screamed as he forced his hand around, felt hers twist against it, sliding to catch her knife with his guard and snap it. The shattered blade caught him above the eye as it flashed past, a spray of red blinding him. He lost his footing for the moment it took Jalina to spin in the haze of water, up to her knees now, one leg out and coming up to connect a kick that nearly broke his jaw.

He blacked out for a moment. Fought his way back to consciousness even as his own knife dropped from his hand to hit the water with a dead-black splash. Jalina was there, dropping to hands and knees with a shout of triumph, but the blade was already beyond her reach in the dark water. Charan stumbled through the fast-flowing surge of the sea, tried to grab his sister, but she was rolling away from him, wet silk like oil against her lean body as sharpened fingernails raked his face.

He swung at her, missed beneath her subtle movement as she spun again and drove her fist into his side, just missing the tight knot of nerves that would have dropped him. They shifted past each other, clumsy and freezing in the rising water as they attacked hand to hand, neither managing to land a blow, their moves too familiar. From the long years of training, from the shorter time of the dark trysts in the White Tower's empty halls, each of their bodies was a map that the other knew too well.

Their father's corpse was floating, a slick of blood spreading across the oily blackness of the thrashing tide. The evenlamp was underwater, its golden light cut to a rippling silver sheen across dark walls. Even in the grim shadows that the body threw to the ceiling, Charan could see that the ladderway was all but gone beneath the roar of dark water at the inflow, no way to even get close enough to climb it now. Before the inflow, the ancient corpse had been torn apart by pressure, blasted to a shadow-swirling storm of bone and rotting cloth.

And in that ancient figure's fractured hands, previously unseen where the shroud of dust and cobwebs had hidden them, a pair of bare-bladed daggers gleamed in the evenlamp's faint glow.

As one, they moved. Charan got there first, only to have Jalina drive the full force of her fist into the side of his neck as his focus drifted from her for just a moment. He saw a haze of red, felt the cold as he hit the water, but then something warm was in his hand and he was up, thrashing side to side to clear wet hair from his eyes.

His sister stood across from him, brown eyes unblinking, a dagger in her hand to match the one in his. Razor-edged stilettos, each set with a wickedly clawed blood-edge that looked as if it might saw through bone with enough force behind it. Their twisted guards were shaped to suggest the flow of water, each set with a diamond at its heart, but one gleaming black, the other brilliant white.

In Jalina's hand, the metal of the dagger was the blue-white of the hottest forge fire, glowing now as if it was fresh-struck in her living grasp. The blade that Charan held tight was black steel that seemed to mark the emptiness between them, unwavering in his hand despite the pain and the blood-dark haze still hanging at the edge of his sight.

The water was at his groin now, his legs numb as the two of them held there, an arm's breadth apart. Both ready to move with the final strike that would spell the end.

Charan felt a strength surge through him then. He felt all the rage, all the uncertainty that had been set in his heart, all of it focused and made sharper. He felt the weight of his father's death leave him, felt the pain of his sister's love torn away like a shroud of leaves on the wind. He felt nothing, felt everything. Felt alive. Jalina's eyes blazed, her teeth set in a hissing smile that told him she felt it, too.

Charan felt something touch him, felt a bond he couldn't explain stretch out across that empty space of longing and laughter and pain. Something stronger even than the forbidden thirst of the blood and the mind that brought them to the tower earlier that night, then brought them to this black-water tomb.

When he was nine years old, he had slipped into the Red Tower of courtly magic by dark to steal two talismans from a young vizier just graduated from the apprentice's suites. Charan knew the relics would be missed, of course, but he had already planted rumors of a taste for gambling and the temple virgins in the vizier's name. After a well-placed bribe to the castellan's office saw the young mage arrested, Charan made a point of not paying attention to his particularly unpleasant fate.

For almost a year, he waited for a night of full Darkmoon rising blood-red with no light of Clearmoon in the sky, as the crumbling scroll that accompanied the pieces in their leather case had bade him. When the time came, he drugged the servants outside his sister's rooms, stole into Jalina's bedchamber. He slipped one of the frail star-silver pieces beneath her pillow.

Then all that endless night, as he had longed to do since he was old enough to remember thought itself, Charan slipped inside his sister's dreams.

A sudden rush of understanding swept through his mind with the force of the sea, surging toward his waist.

In his hand, along his arm, in his ear and mind and only for him, the black blade sang.

Power threaded through him, touching and amplifying the power of the white blade as its own song rose. It was a thing beyond words, beyond thought. A power he and his sister shared suddenly, a nexus of energy that threaded through them. Their bodies turned to silk, scoured by the warm desert wind.

The haze that was all that remained of the broken body was a faint outline beneath the water, but even as his gaze flicked there, Charan was moving suddenly, faster than thought. He sensed a blur of blades, felt twin arcs of white and shadow slash between them as he and Jalina struck, parried, a fast strike caught and spun off a crossguard, the return seeking flesh and striking empty air, again and again.

His vision sharpened in the darkness, a warmth flooding through him. But even as it did, he heard his own voice harsh in his head. *Fool,* he called himself, and a chill twisted through him, helped him focus.

Smarter men than he had felt their lives cut short by the dark dweomer of a cursed blade. Relics left for the finding by those their fell magic had already killed.

He felt the passage of time slow around him. Felt a wholeness that filled his mind and forced out all thought but the memory of that perfect connection he once felt between his sister and himself.

He saw Jalina start as if she sensed his thought. He heard her voice, but in the haze of shadow that suddenly shrouded his sight, his mind, he couldn't be sure whether she spoke, or whether it was her very act of thought tracing through him, or whether he dreamed it in the end.

"Whatever you thought it was, you were wrong."

He parried, spun the black blade through a feint as a blur of shadow, struck hard as he slipped beneath Jalina's return strike. He felt the flesh and bone of her breast yield with the softness of sand. But even as it did, pain like white-hot fire flared at his own chest, and a blade that wasn't there shattered his collarbone and drenched his freezing-wet shirt with a gout of hot blood.

As he had tried and failed to do ever since that dark night, Charan remembered. As he tried to do each time he pulled the shadow over the two of them, slipping into the wordless space where they were one, he felt that wonder of touching his sister's mind.

Charan screamed, scrambling back as his blade pulled free from Jalina. His hand was locked to the haft by searing pain, teeth set against it. His sister's pale face was a mask of fear as she fought her way back through the flood, clutching at the jagged rent in her tunic to reveal no blood there, the pale skin unbroken.

Charan fought to stay on his feet, pressed his shaking knife hand hard to the gash at his chest. He had struck the fast blood, no way to staunch the wound that should have been his sister's, the black blade turning the blow back against himself with all the strength it had borne. The dark dweomer, he thought. But stronger even than the fear of that magic was the knowledge that the blow he had taken would have killed his sister had it struck.

He remembered his father's rage at the tower door. Remembered seeing that same rage too many times to count, a lifetime of anger that was his legacy. He remembered the reflection of that anger, bright in the last light of his father's eyes when the blade left his hand.

Jalina's eyes were wet, her voice all but lost against the roar of water, lapping at her breast now.

"Brother," she called. "Some of us are fated to follow."

She hesitated just long enough to let Charan understand that she knew what she was doing. His utter betrayal of her was the only thing that mattered to her now, as she lunged forward to plunge the length of the gleaming blade into his heart.

Charan felt something twist in his chest, felt his breath stolen away. He saw Jalina's shift suddenly turn black in the shadows, a blood-flower blossoming there in time with his own pulse as she fell.

The roar of water swallowed his scream as it swallowed her body, slipping like a stone beneath the foam. Charan felt the pain at his chest surge as he pushed forward, but then it was gone and replaced by a sharper agony that twisted from gut to heart to head, pounding now with the strength of his own blood and a fear he had never known before.

He was blind in the surge of water and shadow as he fought to dive. He felt her, lost her. Grasped her again by the edge of her shift and hung on to seize her fiercely, fighting the current.

He pulled his sister up from the darkness, screamed her name this time, but her empty eyes were blank. Desperate, he slung her to his shoulders, unaware of her weight as he looked to the ladderway but saw it already gone, the vents submerged where black water boiled.

Behind him, against the last grey flare before the light from below was swallowed, he saw the faintest flicker of firelight. There, beyond the shattered ceiling where the ancient body had once hidden.

Each slow step was agony as Charan fought his way through the freezing inflow, aware that the bitter cold staunching his bleeding was the only reason he was still on his feet. He tried to feel some sign of Jalina's breath where her face was slumped against his, but his vision was a pounding haze, red shadow roaring in his ears. At the ragged opening where the grate had been, he felt his way along the wall as water poured past and out through the ancient drain, threatening to sweep him off his feet.

All was darkness. Then from the passageway that had been sealed came the faint glimmer again. Charan pushed Jalina up, followed close behind her lifeless body into the narrow darkness. He didn't remember climbing, his sister slung across his back as he pushed himself up a narrow chimney of dusty stone and cobwebs. The gleam ahead grew steadily brighter, the red flicker of firelight calling him on even as his mind slipped closer to shadow. He felt the names of all Jalina's dead gods slip unbidden to his mind as he prayed.

His legs were numb, feet bleeding where they gripped rough stone when he arrived at the end of the chute. The glow he followed was blazing bright now, a perfect lozenge of firelight forced through a haze of dust that billowed with his frantic breathing. A keyhole, it looked like. The bottom side of a concealed trapdoor, unlatching easily with a shoulder's pressure from below.

Bright braziers hung by golden chains where Charan pushed himself through. The air was a shimmer of heat haze, darkness claiming him for a moment, but then he was back. Jalina's body sprawled alongside him where he collapsed silently to a floor of night-cold stone. He couldn't see, couldn't feel anything beyond where he groped with shaking fingers for the blood at his sister's throat, found only stilled silence.

He was in the sepulcher, he realized. His sight was shadow and the braziers' faint golden smoke, everburning with the spellcraft of the silent priests. The great tomb of khanans on the lowest level of the castle. Its vaulted columns of white marble held up a ceiling of shimmering black stone brought here a thousand years before from the Mountains of the Moons, far eastward and overlooking the end of the world at the edge of the Great Sea of Storms. His father's ashes would have been laid here, once. Now, they would burn an empty bier, scattered only with the signs and objects of his reign, ready to be reclaimed in the next life that all the dead gods promised.

Charan had been here last when his mother died. Though he told himself he should have known which space was hers among the lines of narrow upright ash-vaults lining the walls to both sides, he couldn't recall it anymore.

From that first night he and Jalina shared, that night of dreams that had inspired the hunger of all the nights that followed, Charan remembered his own face in his sister's mind. Remembered the longing for him that struck his heart like some god's ghostly fist, left him limp and sweat-soaked in the darkness when he awoke.

On that night when he walked in Jalina's dreams, the talisman had turned to ash on his pillow, as he had been warned it would. He squeezed those burning embers in his hand as though he might have willed them to reshape themselves again, tears flowing and body aching. Suddenly crippled beneath a weight he had always carried but never felt before.

With shaking hands, he tore the blood-soaked shift from his sister's body. He pressed hard at the jagged wound the white blade's magic had torn at her breast, but her flesh was ice.

On the floor beside him, the black and white steel of the twin daggers caught the flickering light.

Charan felt his breath cut off suddenly. He stared.

He didn't remember slipping the weapons to his belt. Didn't remember even seeing the gleaming white steel of the blade with which Jalina had taken her life. He must have grabbed it even as she fell, he thought. But he couldn't have. Must have been holding it the entire time without realizing. Impossible.

Carefully, he reached for them. First one, then the other. He felt their warmth as they slipped into his shaking hands, left and right, white and black. And without thinking, without understanding, he shifted to press the pale blade into Jalina's unfeeling grasp.

As it did before, the silver-white dagger began to glow. A shimmering ghost light, the mottled ice-sheen of his sister's dead flesh.

Charan felt a trace of faint energy thread his trembling fingers, suddenly stilled as it flowed through them and up his arm. When it reached his chest, the pain there flared again to remind him how he had forgotten it. But then it slowed. Stopped.

Where his sister sprawled before him, he saw the jagged wound at her heart slowly close within its shroud of blood.

Charan had felt the power of the healing magic before, the animyst-priests of his father's court ministering to him when he shattered his leg in a childhood fall from the White Tower roof. He had seen the rites of returning only once. A captain of his father's was brought back from beyond the veil of death, struck down in combat but deemed too valuable to be left to that darkness. He died again less than a year later. Took his own life, the stories said, driven mad by what he had seen in that shadow before the light returned.

Charan's eyes were wet, breath coming ragged as he saw his sister's fingers flinch against the cold haft of the white blade in her hand. Her skin was silk smooth, all the marks of their dark labor in the sewer washed away.

As he watched, Jalina shuddered, convulsed once as she vomited blood and black water and her eyes opened wide. The wound at her breast was closed, the pale perfect skin sealed over without so much as a mark. She stared up, meeting Charan's gaze where he loomed over her, trembling. He fumbled for her soaked tunic, found one corner cleaner than the rest and gently washed the slick of blood from her face and neck.

Shaking, she raised herself up to kiss him hard, wrap herself in his arms.

They stayed that way for a long while, and when their clothes had dried well enough in the braziers' golden heat, they slipped back through the deep-night castle, then to the secret ways only they knew that led past the servants and to their separate chambers. The same secret ways that had taken them to the White Tower, a lifetime ago now. The ghost blade was clutched tight to Jalina's breast, the dagger whose darkness was the endless night in Charan's hand when their other hands reluctantly parted at last. Fingers slipping from each other, they went their separate ways without a word.

Apart, Charan waited, watching and dozing at the high windows that opened up to the great green-garden courtyard across from his sister's suites. First dawn touched the gleaming towers of the city, twisted the shroud of shadow to a veil of gold across the sky and the star-shining black of the bay.

He remembered the night of shared dreams. From the dark shelter of his own slumber, he walked inside Jalina's mind, feeling the song her thought made, seeing the bright desert dawn that was the backdrop to all her fear and youthful longing.

He felt her dreams and the warmth of a kindling passion he had never felt before. He remembered his own face seen in her mind's eye. Remembered what it felt like to love and be loved that way.

He felt the hunger that had so long twisted through him finally settle and shape itself to something else. He was dreaming of Jalina, the day breaking blue and bright beneath a cloudless sky, when the frantic knock came at the door and the rest of their lives began.

— The Game of **Heart** and **Light** —

SHE IS LYING beneath the pear trees along the high slope of the back garden when the Magician Prince appears, sluiced in shadow that unfurls and spills to soak the ground. A dark stain spreads, fades as the rush of air swirls in the wake of his apparition and his voice rings out amidst the green.

Stay with me always, Pale Princess.

A flight of titmice in the high branches are shocked from the drowsy torpor of the eternal autumn sun, gangling to the air on the strength of shrill voices and blue-black wings. The wind snips darkening leaves from the trees, one by one, their autumn red the color of the Prince's flowing hair, the narrow beard, the brows arched above steel-grey eyes.

The caress of sun-warmed grass beneath her neck, her naked arms. She looks up at the gentle figure looming over her, whose loving expression tells her of the longing with which he waits for her to take the shelter of his embrace. But the grey eyes are seized with uncertain pain when he sees that she is weeping instead, and as the tears fall, she knows not why.

"Show me the way home," she says, fading hope resonant in her voice like the echo of birdsong across the sky.

She lifts to her feet with all the lightness of her young form. She leaps to the air to retrieve two pears whose flesh is the golden-brown of brushed calfskin, the scent of honeysuckle and summer dawn.

To the trembling Magician Prince, she hands one sun-ripened fruit. She bites the other, letting its cool sweetness stifle her sadness as she skips across the lawn, then breaks to a run.

She hears him call out behind her, but she is already gone. Then the garden has another statue, a tall figure wrapped in a skirl of cloak, arms outstretched where he reached for her at the end.

The golden pear and the hand that holds it are white marble. The autumn-sweet scent still swirls, set within the Prince's fast-fixed fingers. The other grasping hand is frozen in an arc of movement, embracing the invisible touch of the wind. And all the while, she runs. Not wanting to look, her mind focused on the future. Looking beyond the past that freezes into place behind her.

All that day, she runs the vine-strewn paths of garden and glade. And as the sun sets, she plays the game of Heart and Light. Retracing all the moments, all the movement, all the pieces of the past so that she might set a new course for that past. Might turn away from what has always been.

The back garden opens onto rocky slopes of heather and flowering thorn, set with white petals of blood-flecked pollen, russet leaves rustling at the endless turning of the season. The stream flows around and past great breakers of tumbled stone, and she follows its path with familiar steps while the sun is warm, following the laughing waters on their endless course that has no beginning, no end. The same as the stair-wall of the garden that she walks at dawn and sunset, ever-climbing the great circle of its path along the walls when she greets the day, then descending back along the same course as the night falls and she dances her way forever down.

In the grey marble courtyard, the Prince of Justice finds her slipping from the white shift of the day's garden to a whisper-shroud of night-dark silk girdled with golden vines, the same as she sets to her dark hair. He is tall and fair, bedecked in mail of dwyrsilver set with studs of apple-red jasper. These match the gems that mark sword-hilt and helm, gleaming with dweomered light that reflects the color of the flowing hair, the narrow beard, the brows arched above steel-grey eyes.

Thou hast come for me, Pale Princess, he says with the longing of a confession lost through endless years, *and hast always come, and will save me from this moment until the end of time...*

He draws the sword whose blade gleams the dull grey of adamant, swings it around him in fury to slash the well-shaped tangles of clematis whose twisting surge takes them up and around fluted columns of black and white marble. The grass at his boots is close-cropped green, edged with viola and sun-bright honeysuckle.

"Show me the way home," she whispers. A shrug of her shoulders and a broken smile. Then he is gone to stillness, cast in stone like all the rest.

She remembers the day they loved. "Never leave me," she says. An echo. An image. A vision that breaks through all the armor of memory and longing, but still she cannot see his face, cannot know his name.

His hand is in hers as they walk along the colonnade, as they stride upon the rocky slopes of heather and he whispers to her of love. "You are my Heart and Light," comes his voice to her shadowed ear, "and shall always be." His fingers are tight in the dark tresses of her hair, and she feels the magic of that moment cut through her as a pale blade.

She remembers the night they loved, the starlit bower, their bodies entwined. And as she sits in the bower now and the memory fades, vanishes back in time, never was, the Fair Prince comes to her. In hunting breeches and leather shirt, a bow across his back and face burned brown by sun and wind, he tries to catch her up in his broad arms.

Thou hast waited for me, Pale Princess, the Fair Prince says in pain, *casting thy heart to pale effigies, watching blindly...*

She feels herself drowning in the flowing hair that is the color of the bower's blanket-floor of maple leaves, kissing the lips that chill and change and then are stone suddenly, and he is gone. Lost to the quick snap of time that closes around him like the heart-vine blossoms squeezing shut on the night. A skein of white stars wheels, twisting silken across the black sky.

"Show me the way home," she says quietly, but the blank eyes simply stare, the polished marble of his face agleam in the starlit dark.

That night, she plays the game of Heart and Light.

She finds herself in the necropolis of white marble and black jade, discovering again as she has so many times before the torchlit stair at the garden's end. Its first discovery was long ago now, far back in her endless memory so that she cannot recall a time before the stair, yet she knows that such a time once was. The light of steel cressets burns cool white as she descends, slippered feet passing with the silence of the night.

Down and down the stair falls, turning and twisting like ivy, dark like the shroud of her hair, gleaming black in the pale light. Turning and twisting and straightening finally to lead her to the great field of gravestones with their ranks of empty names, and the shimmering silver mist that floats between them, shifting and flowing like leaves that kiss the surface of the stream.

The pieces of the game of Heart and Light are movement and song as she approaches, shifting through their delicate dance whose flickering pace shivers the mirror-mist on which they hang suspended, sends shadows spinning along the torch-bright air. They are figures carved of jet and bluestone, bleached bone and living wood. They are tugged by spider-silk anchoring faint breezes, lit by motes of fire and lightning that dance beneath the pressure of her breath. They are lives and deaths and choices made that circle in shifting patterns, marking out the passage of a world long passed.

And in the endless patterns of that shifting, she knows there lies a single motif yet unseen. A thousand thousand configurations of life and anger, hope and dreams, the voices of peoples long dead that ring out for her ears alone now. Subtle shiftings of her fingers, her words, her thoughts set the pieces in motion, restart a life long lost in the hope that it might twist away from the dark end that she will not think about.

But each time, the game plays out the same. Shadow falls at dawn as the torches flicker and fade, and she is dancing up the stairs without knowing why, without knowing where they lead, until at last their pale stones spill out once more into the sun.

From before, she recalls the scent of roses. White and red and blue in bright fans, sweet-scented against dew-kissed stone walls. She stands upon the portico now, sheltered in the shadow of a vine-grown pillar behind a pearl-shimmer haze of rain. She remembers his hand in hers as she passes along ivory-graveled paths, beneath sweeping arbor arches whose living arms of willow shimmer gold in the wind.

"Show me the way home," she says, only to herself.

Are you ready…?

As night falls and the moons'-light rises, the statues that stand in ranks along garden and lawn are weeping, their faces shimmering as each is scoured by a sheen of tears. But when she remembers, she remembers that these are her tears, shed for a sorrow she can no longer name. A storm's breath of sadness with which she covers each face like a shroud, because she knows that to gaze on them all at once would tell her a thing that she cannot ever know.

Are you ready…?

She hears the voice this night for the first time, but it is different than the first times of all her other understandings. The bower of her garden, tressed with coppice branches gleaming white. The colonnade of statues twisting out and down across night-kissed glade to the even more distant shadows. These are things seen and sensed for so many first times. Always remembered in each passing glance, then forgotten when her gaze strays away, then to be remembered again.

The voice is different. The voice is new, slipping in through the chill of all that is old, all that is safe, all that surrounds her.

Are you ready…?

The voice is a woman's. Not the deep longing tones of all her Princes, their words red-gold and bright like the hair that holds the light of sunset, the pursed lips set within the close-trimmed beard, from which come the words of passion and an endless longing lost to time.

This is different.

Something has changed.

The game of Heart and Light is the name she gives it. If it has another name, she knows it not. The game of Heart and Light has rules that she does not understand. Not yet.

Not yet.

Through the shadows, the woman's voice rings out chime-bright, but the Pale Princess turns away.

She remembers the day they met, his hand seeking hers across a ballroom floor. The eyes of seneschals and nobles, frowning court wizards, her mother and father follow them within the crowd, the surge of dance and laughter and golden light with which the night is painted. The same dance that the figures of the game make now as she watches, stone and bone and wood skating in subtle arcs within the silvered mist. She does not remember how she came down the stairs. She does not remember when she finally goes.

As hard as she tries to follow the dance, as hard as she tries to judge its motion, shape its flow, each flick of her hand and thought pushes the game of Heart and Light beyond the music she whispers, beyond the time she craves to set. As hard as she tries to follow, as intently as she watches the dance for the signs of the ending she fears, that ending comes. Inexorable. Spiteful.

Without knowing the how or why, she feels the knowledge well up in her for a moment, an instant, a brief flicker of time. Then her hand darts within the dance, shifting more pieces, hopeful. Her breath comes unseen and up close, as her hollow laugh sends an unseen storm to spiral cloud and fire and lightning away into new places, new patterns that quickly ripple outward.

There is a pattern that must be found. There is a code to the game of Heart and Light that will unlock the dance of puzzle pieces, and which will let time be rewritten.

She remembers. Forgets.

She remembers. The day they wed, the scent of roses. The crowns set on her head and his glimmer silver-gold like sunlight on water, the cheering of a faceless crowd and the weight of history and history to come set on their young shoulders. Then the memory is gone and a blade twists in her breast and the woman's voice calls to her.

Not yet.

She is walking upon the moss green, fingers tracing the bright stone of curving walls when the air splits and splinters, and the Golden Prince is there. She knows him as she knows them all in the instant of seeing. Remembering suddenly the past and present as it unfolds. Remembering the aura of his shimmering robes, the bright eyes of grey, the flowing hair like the light of last sunset, his hand reaching for hers.

Thou wilt never abandon me, Pale Princess, he says. *Thou wilt fight the forces of fate to stay eternal at my side.*

She smiles to see him because she must smile. Because she is a piece in the game of Heart and Light, feeling the tug of the dance her song makes, that her love makes as she watches the movement of other milling figures bright upon their shimmering sea.

This much she knows. The game of Heart and Light is a game that she must win.

"Show me the way home," she whispers, and the figure of white and gold that she knows but cannot name unfurls his arms for her to fall within, an endless embrace.

Then he is stilled like all the rest, and stands to watch the sun pass by behind her as she dances. So that in the movement of her sun-warmed limbs, the sadness might be cast away.

"Show me the way home," she whispers, because she understands, just for a moment.

Through the day where she rests in her rose bower, she hears the slow and steady song of the game of Heart and Light deep within the ground, the regular clockwork whisper timed to her heartbeat as she sings. As the days twist on, the song stays steady beneath the whisper of wind and sun. Walking the blossom-white paths that wend between apple trees, each step echoes with the bright ring of mirrored glass.

Each night's placement of pieces shatters itself by dawn. Each arrangement of possibilities in the game of Heart and Light splits and shivers and is no more. She hears the song where she kneels in the necropolis of marble and jade, lingering by the gravestones and the gnarled trees from which the pieces of the game are carved, discarded, carved again.

She hears it again as morning turns to later days, walking the ever-lengthening course of the statues that are her suitors. To each of their tear-streaked faces, she offers a smile in turn, letting their words slip to the air for just a moment from the iron grip of time.

Thou hast come for me, the Prince of Justice says.

Stay with me always, calls the Magician Prince.

Hold me through all time, says the Dancing Prince.

Thou wilt never abandon me, the Golden Prince cries.

Thou hast waited for me, says the Fair Prince, time and time and time again.

Thou will holdest me, calls the Prince of Blades, quick of movement where he appears along the wall below the colonnade, scaling up toward her like a cat. He clings to crumbling columns and sings her name as a song of sunlight and escape, but soon enough, the song ends. A sad last note whispers past still lips, the grey eyes paled with the cold of timelessness and loss.

"Show me the way home…" She whispers it as she slips away to the shadowed stairs, a blur of unspoken words in her mind. Her thoughts change shape, unfurling like strawflower petals sending spiked fingers forth to taste the rain.

"Show me the way home," the voice comes in answer, and she sees the Sorceress. Another in an endless line of first times stretching back through all times.

The Sorceress's hair is dark and hangs to shroud her pale face. The Sorceress' eyes lurk unseen in shadow as she steps forth, into the midst of play pieces shifting across their foundations of mirrored mist.

She is in the necropolis of white marble and black jade, has been there forever, cannot remember ever setting foot beyond its crumbling stairs. She watches the Sorceress, feels the game of Heart and Light unfold around her, its song of possibility crashing to discord, twisting as shattered-glass echoes in her mind.

"Do you remember?" the Sorceress asks, her voice steel-edged with quiet uncertainty. The importance of the question, the cadence of her own answer, will determine whether the Sorceress's mission here succeeds or fails, the Pale Princess realizes. She knows this with perfect clarity. She does not understand.

"Show me the way home…"

The words hang above the bright world in her own voice, in the voice of the Sorceress. She does not understand.

The Sorceress kisses her, and she feels the mirrored pieces of a lost past refract and fracture and set themselves anew within her mind.

Then as she has again, as she will before, she watches as the garden falls.

She watches as gleaming columns of vine-twined marble flake and flitter away, splitting along a dozen, a hundred, a thousand fault lines as they collapse and crumble to splintered shards, to rubble, to sand and ash.

She watches the stream turn back on itself, its flow and clear sound twisting, folding to gloom, vanishing in a shimmer of black steam and the plaintive cry of rain swallowed by the burning air. She sees the trees wither and fall, leaves contracting to bare white branches, branches fading to buds that dark-stipple slender trunks, which shrink back into the earth that bore them, which swallows the seeds that trees once were, which swirls downward as twisting gouts of dust.

She watches the Sorceress sing, hears that song echo along the colonnade of statues that wear the face she cannot remember, cannot forget. And one by one, their porcelain ears, their marble lips take up that song and the magic of its words and tune.

"Show me the way home..."

• • •

She was lying beneath black arches that rose as rune-carved pillars to a murky ceiling overhead. The couch beneath her was marble-carved, set with no cushion or cloak to be betrayed to rot by the passage of time. She was naked, curled around the empty space of chill air like a babe at a mother's vanished breast. The ache of cold stone twisted through her as she rose up, fell to the floor and her knees with the spasm of muscles frozen by the passage of endless years of time.

The dank shadows of the tomb rose around her. The Sorceress was gone.

Flitting into memory, half-imagined visions of the past. Around the walls, evenlamps glowed with cold flame, carving out pools of pale light whose edges intersected each other, made curved scars of brighter white that marked the chamber like the claws of time. Pinning down this moment in its endlessness, pinning her down as she dragged her way forward toward a black pool, set as a perfect square within the center of the floor.

She lifted herself shakily to kneel along an edge of marble tile, stared down into dark water. Mirror-still even where four fonts spilled streaming at each far corner, ripples spreading and deadened and vanished in an unnatural silent flow.

She remembered. She felt the fear set a tremble to her lips, her dry eyes.

She heard the voice of the Dead Prince in her mind.

Stay with me always, Pale Princess.

On the sarcophagus that rose along the pool's far side, she saw the relief-carved likeness of that voice's noble face. Its flowing hair and narrow beard were etched in ivory, the brows arched above stone-blank eyes.

"You are my Heart and Light," she said to the darkness, "and shall always be."

Stay with me always, Pale Princess.

"You are dead," she whispered.

Stay with me always, Pale Princess.

"I have fought the forces of fate, but you are gone…"

Along the walls, she saw painted the bright garden where they had once walked, pear and apple trees hanging heavy beneath endless autumn, above green lawn that edged courtyard and bower and stair-wall, the laughing stream twisting beneath clouds held on faint breezes, sun and moons circling overhead.

"I remember," she said, and she did.

She remembered the day they met, his hand seeking hers across a ballroom floor.

She remembered the day they loved, his hand in hers as they walked along the colonnade.

She remembered the day they wed, the scent of roses, crowns glimmering silver-gold.

She remembered the day he died, consumed by a hail of black spell-fire on distant battlefields, when his spirit died with him. No imprint of his brief life left behind him, no animys to call back from the darkness. And in her grief, in her madness, she would tell herself that if she could not live with him, she would spend all of timeless eternity in the game of Heart and Light. Remembering.

She remembered the curse that she herself had laid within this space of sealed stone, an ancient spell of immortal time gleaned from long-forgotten grimoires, practiced and paid for in coin and blood and the remaining long years of her life. Artisans and laborers pledged the strength of minds and muscled bodies to the construction of the crypt, its location chosen atop a well of dark mana. And when it was done, she drew upon that magical energy which would fuel a ripple in time. A ritual of eternity, binding her to past and memory.

"Are you ready?"

Where light and shadow played along the still surface of the pool, she stared down to see the Sorceress there.

"I have shown you the way home..."

The voice was a whisper of pain, threading the muffled shadows where frozen time stilled the surface of the water as she touched it with a shaking hand. The ripples of her movement were swallowed by nothingness, by the mana that permeated air and stone, light and shadow. From the black pool, the pale eyes stared back, dark hair framing the face through which the pain of remembering twisted like unseen worms beneath the skin.

"Not yet," she said.

Each time, the game plays out the same.

There is a pattern that must be found. There is a code to the game of Heart and Light that will let time be rewritten.

She remembers. Forgets.

"Never leave me," she whispers the day they loved. "Never leave me," she whispers later in the starlit bower, their bodies entwined, spirits spilling through each other, and she realizes that this is a power greater than the arcane fire of her blood and her life's studies, greater than the radiant power of animys, greater than the energy of life that binds all the world.

Greater than the magic she had spent her whole life searching for, and which she shaped and honed and used to consume that life in the end.

"Never leave me," she whispered now, and the stone couch was cold against her cheek as the darkness slipped down around her and she was gone.

• • •

She is lying beneath the pear trees along the high slope of the back garden when the Dancing Prince appears, taking her hand to an unseen music spilling through the trill of birdsong and the gentle whistle of the winds. His raiment is velvet and spider-silk, his cloak a swirl of ivory and cloth-of-gold that holds the song of the air and whispers it back in all the endless voices that are his.

Hold me through all time, Pale Princess, he says, and her laughter adds a counterpoint to the song they make together and have always made, his smile bright as the sun whose setting is the red of his flowing hair, the narrow beard, the brows arched above grey eyes. But as he sweeps her across the grey marble courtyard, as she feels the red carpet of bower floor and the green lawn of shimmering statues beneath her feet, her hand is trembling and she knows not why.

"Show me the way home..." she says.

— Shadow to **Shadow** —

THE DISTANCE FROM THE RIVER to the fane was measured as nearly a thousand paces along the twisting line of the road, a little less than half that distance in a straight line through the hilly grasslands through which the rutted farm track swept. The sun was up, pale where it gilded the haze of green. Conry ran through summer grass, following the twisting trails already filling in where sheep had wandered the winter before.

It was early still, the short time that marked the change from night's cool to warmth of day. Overhead was darkness. Behind him, the dawn. Conry had seen twelve summers pass, and he possessed in him the strength of leg that only the long summer gave as he raced past cottonwood grove and fieldstone fence, watching his shadow stretch before him as the sun rolled slowly upward against the level plane of sky behind.

Lady Jeslyn was gone to the gods, and feeling the shadow of that departure made him savor the new heat of morning, warming his arms and back through white homespun. Where rough stands of witch-willow grew tall, shadows swallowed each other and turned the ground to grey, breaking where Conry parted them with his passage and allowed the golden light to bleed through.

Lady Jeslyn was dead.

Where the scrubland broke to open range on one hand and forest on the other, the fane rose in the shadow of the southern hills. On the barren crest of the road, the air swirled the grey-black of late-night sky, dust rising, the color of old leather. Each night, the dew kissed the ground in a web of crystal, but now it had already begun to vanish again in the sun's light. Spread out to a shimmering haze, that light twisted with the dust in whisper-thin clouds stirred by the passage of a hay wain, by the footsteps of a slow-walking woodcutter who gave to Conry a slow nod of recognition.

The sky was clear and growing hotter and had been for five days now, and all the folk of the village and the farms feared what that might mean.

Old Rhen it was who had called down the rains since before Conry was born, but Old Rhen, too, was dead. His body was found the same morning that Lady Jeslyn was found, but his was the godless way of the druidas and there would be no rites for him except the cairn the farm folk had quietly raised.

They named his killer as some unknown beast that must have fled along the river that night, the hunter patrols finding no trace of its tracks. Then even more quietly, a few spoke careful litanies in the old druid's name, fearing for the season to come when no magic would channel the thin clouds in their high passage, streaming west toward the flank of the mountains from the distant sea. Old Rhen it was who had spoken with the voice of tree and field and all the creatures that dwelt there. Old Rhen who died whispering of the old magic for Conry's ear alone, because there was no one else to hear.

Lady Jeslyn was dead, and Old Rhen was dead, and everything had changed.

The night before, Conry had slept a fitful sleep of summer heat, and of the pain still rooting deep in the healers' scars whose pale lines marked his arm. He stretched loose along the length of the pallet that was nearly too small for him now, woolen blanket piled unneeded at his feet, sweat stippling his forehead, his chest, the small of his back. He woke once from the silver web of dreams and heard the usual sound. Footsteps.

His father was in the hall beyond the bedchambers, pacing as he did so many nights. Returning home from long days at the fane, or at one of the neighboring farmsteads where his healing skill and the power of the gods was needed, Conry's father continued to move through the shadows of the house he had built with his own hands. Walking the night away.

Conry had seen eight summers pass when his mother died. He remembered his father began his pacing then, that faint sound and image fixed in his mind alongside the memory of his mother's rites. She had been lost to a sickness that not even his father's hands administering the grace of Crecinu the healer could cure, as those hands could not cure Lady Jeslyn in the end. But as much as he searched for them, night after night in dreams, Conry had no memories of his mother beyond the rites. Nothing earlier. No sense of who she had been before going to the gods.

He closed his eyes, following his father's route in the darkness of his mind. He saw him looking, staring out through white-framed shutters into the depths of the black grasslands, to catch a sight of something in a night whose darkness held no trace of image.

He had gone to his father four mornings past to have the wounds at his arm healed, and had lied and described the rocks that had slashed at him when he fell along the riverbank. His father set the magic of animys in him, then admonished him, and Conry knew and gave silent thanks that there was no memory in his father of the night Lady Jeslyn died.

The footsteps left the window, started up again. The same route retraced. Conry drifted back slowly to the shadow, the state of welcome sleep blurring with the haze that the heat created in his mind. When his father finally stopped pacing, he couldn't hear.

In the broad field alongside the fane, in the light of midmorning, more carts and wagons stood idle than Conry had seen there on a single day in all the years of his memory. The carts had set out from the farmsteads when he did, tracking the rising sun and setting gales of dust behind them as they made their way slowly from a half-dozen directions. Now, the last of their passengers were crossing the field, through the dust of the dry lane and up to where the high front doors of the fane were open wide. From across the village and from all the houses around, from the small farmsteads and the tracks that stretched out in the shadow of the trade road, they had all come.

More carts had reached the fane this day than the narrow space of the lane could handle, and so they spilled out onto the grass and along the road beyond. Farm wains and gigs, mule carts and empty wagons were laid out in rows, bleached wood cracked and canvas furling in the faint breeze. Horses were hitched to weathered posts or to other wagons where the posts ran out, the somber grey of the ground clinging to hooves and legs and wheels like an unshifting shadow.

Still more had come on foot. Most of the younger folk, trudging silently along the twisting track to the village. Everyone in the village, everyone who had ever called the village home was there. They came even from the distant orchard farms, along the broad road to Damiadi and Brin that ran through green fields and stretches of pine forest whose scent carried on the wind.

Conry had never walked the road beyond the village, but he sensed the distant forest as he felt the wind push from the east again. In the outlying ranks of carts and gigs, he saw the telltale signs that marked the strangers. A certain cleanliness. A fresher patina of dust, more easily washed away.

Inside the narrow space of shadow that the rough stone walls of the fane made, all the devout knelt now with heads bowed and prayers hung on pursed lips for Lady Jeslyn's soul. They pressed close to the brazier and the altar of the Orosana, the twelve gods dwelling in the unseen mountains of the Drachen's Teeth to the north, the nearer peaks of the Shieldcrest shimmering along the southern skyline.

Through the open doors at their backs, the light was a pale blur. The sky beyond was a sun-streaked white, the heat waxing oppressive. Far too many bodies packed far too closely together, the swept flag-stones of the floor cool beneath them. All the side aisles and the back of the nave filled with the dark shapes of figures bent to prayer. All here for this last look, to gaze up upon Lady Jeslyn this final time. To pay the respects that were due.

Lady Jeslyn was dead now, and the High Summer that would have brightly marked Conry's thirteenth year was shrouded by the disquiet of death, hanging like the low mist of morning that the sun too quickly burned away. She had been found in the fane, naked and alone at first light where she must have wandered in her age and infirmity, must have fallen the night before. Conry's father discovered her, but it was the guards of the manor house who carried her home, and Lady Jeslyn's cousins who were her servants who washed her aged flesh, set-ting her to lie quiet in the parlor that overlooked the garden and the fields beyond.

Lady Jeslyn was older than anyone in the village or the farmsteads that surrounded it. Ninety-six summers, Old Rhen's voice in Conry's mind had said. Just as that voice had told how Lady Jeslyn had earned that age, by testing the power of the healers and the potion-masters of distant Brin for half those years or more. Age showed in the lines of her face but had never slowed her, had never bent her back or set its shadow in her eyes.

In the end, though, not even the healers' arts could hold back the time that came for all folk. The darkness and the light beyond, as Con-ry's father named it. The passage from life to death that marks the gods' welcome to what lies ahead.

Lady Jeslyn had changed on a journey she had made to Brin at High Spring, a season past. Old Rhen had whispered it to Conry with a voice already dead. Others had spoken of that trip, though with an idler interest. Lady Jeslyn hated the pace of travel, and so had never left the village for more than a handful of days that anyone could recall. But when she went this time on the long carriage south, she was twenty days away. She said nothing of her business there, but Old Rhen's voice in Conry's mind had spoken of seeing a darkness in her, and the curtains closed always in the upstairs of the manor house from the day she returned.

Conry knew the story as did all in the village, of how the manor and all the village lands around it had been Lady Jeslyn's father's once, and her father's father who was a knight's squire of the Empire and the High King that were both gone. Those lands could be seen from the crest of the low rise where the trade road wound away north for Damiadi. Endless leagues of range grass and snake fence, spread with the shadow of cattle and sheep as far as the eye could follow. The view from the tops of the low-lying hills that Lady Jeslyn would see no more.

The one thing that no one would ever know is what Lady Jeslyn said to the master healers of the temples in the city, when they must have shaken their heads with looks of unknowing sadness and told her there was no more their magic could do.

The one thing no one would ever know is where she went once the master healers turned her away.

The magic that was the power granted Conry's father had held the body in repose until this gods' day, when Lady Jeslyn was prepared to receive the rites of the Orosana. From dusk to dawn over four long nights, his father had been with her in the parlor of the manor house, where the light of candles flickered at the open windows until morning. Conry's father who was the priest of Danassa, goddess of spring, and of all the Orosana. Conry's father who prayed all those nights with Lady Jeslyn's servant-cousins, who were her kin from Valos Duchy to the east, bound by family debts first to her husband's service, then to hers. It was his father who held their hands and told them to feel no sorrow. Told them that a great light shines forth when death comes down like fast nightfall, and that light was the memory of our deeds on earth, and the life that was Lady Jeslyn's had passed before them with the light of cloudless noon on first snow.

Conry was there to hear it, each and every night. He had asked his father's permission to accompany him, but it was not his father's words he came for. Instead, all that dark time, he watched the body with dark eyes and a fear that parched his throat and set his heart hammering in his chest. Lady Jeslyn arrayed on her fine bier, dressed in all the elegance that one would have expected, that she would have demanded while alive. Pale under candlelight by night, as she was pale now by the grey light of the fane's day.

All those nights, her eyes were closed tightly, but not like someone sleeping, Conry thought. More like a person hiding. Trying not to see.

Her gown was black and long, tucked in at the edges of her narrow waist, cuffs pulled down to completely cover the white wrists, hem trailing lace and fine silk. The gown looked cold as deepest night, Conry thought, like Lady Jeslyn herself looked cold. The bier of black oak and cushioned silk was set with delicate trim in white silver and she was framed within it, all immobile, face and features carved of the palest ice.

Lady Jeslyn was barely a child when she married. These were the stories his father and the servant-cousins had told through the long dark of the rites. Lady Jeslyn was barely a woman of twenty when dark fate and the dangers of the frontier worked together to make a widow of her. He was killed on the hunt, he and the guards of the manor who were sworn to him. They had ridden forth to rout trolls that long-ago spring, the foul creatures stealing out from the dread woods of Meginus to ravage outlying farmsteads. When the hunters failed to return, Old Rhen had led the force that tracked them to the site of their destruction, the carcasses of men and horses spread in a dark offering. It had taken two days to collect enough remains for the rites, or so the stories said.

All those years ago, Lady Jeslyn found herself alone with the manor in her name, and so she came to the fane that dark night, on her knees with the fear of all the mortal world in her eyes. It was Conry's grandfather who had first told the story, which Conry's father told again during the four nights of the rites. A story he would tell for the last time during the eulogy to come, speaking of how Lady Jeslyn's blood marked her as a purest daughter of Gracia, but how like all those who had seen the fall of the heathen Empire, she had lived without the true touch of the gods.

That night, she came to Conry's grandfather who was priest before his father, asking for the guidance that only the gods can give. Asking for light that might show her the path to redemption from the legacy that tragedy left her, for she had no one else to turn to.

"I am small," she had said, "and alone in the emptiness that love leaves me," and Conry's grandfather had spoken of taking her by the hand in the fane, the two of them lost in the shadows.

"Learn from the strength inside you," he told her, "for there is no force of pain or death which can come between you and the gods' love.

Behind every mask that death wears, there is a mortal face of life and memory. Beneath every cloak of mourning hides the white robes of hope."

Lady Jeslyn made her peace with the gods that night, as the story told it. Coming wholly into the house of the Orosana for the first time. "In tragedy's mirror," said Conry's father during the rites, "do we see the true face of the gods. Though pain's cold tears blind us, still do all other senses hear redemption's song."

And Conry had listened darkly through all four nights, and in his mind, he heard the voice of Old Rhen who was dead, and he waited.

Three doors opened into the fane to mark the Triad of Brothers. The main doors were Denas the High Father's, a great double expanse of planks cut from lightning-struck oak to mark the storm lord's power. The second door opened beyond the altar stone, which was the strength of Phion, the earth and sea. The third was set beyond the brazier whose disc was the shield of Rhilos, the warrior.

Conry slipped in through the altar door, falling back to watch from the shadows that cloaked the altar stone. Across the fane, the light was already bright through the main doors and the high windows that faced the east, but over the altar and the brazier was pale shadow still. Even against the heat that rose so early outside, the brazier was burning, incense and woodsmoke a thick column that twisted to the high chimney above. The scrub oak that stood beyond the fane's walls of rough-cut granite clustered close-grown and tall, blocking the sun to thin rays of morning light. Above the shrine and the bier before it, the windows were a narrow line of grey.

Lady Jeslyn's cousins who were her servants knelt in that lingering shadow, close to Conry at the altar's edge. Those who had the privilege of calling themselves closest to Lady Jeslyn were just behind. The men somber in dark sash and tunic, swords at their waists that most had not worn in long years. The women in pale shifts, dark veils that hung low and hid their faces, hid the pale gaze of anxious eyes. In the air, the scent of bodies wove in with the scintilla fragrance of the dust, of road-worn cloaks and oiled leather where the house guards of Lady Jeslyn's manor stood ranked by the doors.

Slipping through the hall like faint birdsong, whispers drifted from one ear to another. Secret syllables, words of assurance that Conry picked up only in passing, for he wasn't really listening. Near the bier, cut flowers and orchard blossoms were laid in gentle patterns that suggested a kind of tranquility. The twisting of branches in the wet spring wind, the swirl of uncut grass in midsummer. As the last mourners arrived, Conry watched to see the flowers borne in from outside, bright in the morning light, tied with ribbons and knots of white string. Then they faded somehow within the walls of the fane, the colors dulled as each figure stepped within the pale light through the streaked windows high above.

It was said that Old Rhen had loved Lady Jeslyn before she was married. It was said more quietly that she had loved him in the long years after her husband's death, so that Conry knew the tree-priest by that rumor through all the years of his own childhood, even after Lady Jeslyn's favor was said to have passed the druid by. Even more, though, all knew the reverence and respect the farm folk paid Old Rhen for the rains. The rich croplands, the golden fields, were spread north and east beyond the dark edge of Meginus Forest, and where the village rose along the river would have been hardscrabble scrubland but for the magic of Old Rhen. So the village folk said, but never in the hearing of Conry's father.

This fact he had learned young, hearing the silent undercurrent of talk that shifted like a quickly changing wind when his father passed by. The talk of faith and the talk of life, he had thought it when he was younger. The things that folk will and will not say when they know the gods and their servants are listening.

So it was that Conry had never spoken to Old Rhen until the day the druid died. A chance day of high sun and dry breeze that stirred the dark shroud of dust along the road, taking him to the river where he skipped and sang, and then suddenly stopped to see a figure sitting in the shadows of a great willow whose roots clenched earth and water like claws.

He recognized the druid by his robe of unwashed homespun, and by the lines of black ink that twisted like dark lightning up his arms. Old Rhen sat on the bank in a swirl of green shadow, the sun bright above shimmering willow leaves and surrounding cottonwood that set their white clouds aloft on the breeze. Conry stood and stared for a long while from the shadow of the crooked trail that wound along the river's edge to the fane track, and he was about to creep away when the old man spoke.

"What are you afraid of, boy?"

Conry turned back. "My father tells me to fear you," he said with all the honesty of youth.

"And why would your father tell you to fear an old man?"

"Because your magic is the darkness of druidas."

"And what does that mean indeed?" Old Rhen's dark eyes arched and flickered beneath brows the same granite-grey as his hair, grown long and tied back with a hand's-breadth of grapevine.

"You deny the true faith of the gods," the boy said.

"A wise man denies only that which he neither sees nor hears. So show me your gods, that I might see them and recognize the error of my ways."

"The power of the gods cannot be unseen, old man. It is the works of folk and nature, mind and magic and all that mind and magic create. All the work that we do in this life, we do in the gods' names, and all we are is the sum of the deeds done in their names."

They were his father's words, not his. His father's voice alive in him, and Conry felt the thrill of it. When he was younger, he would kneel at the altar at his father's side and listen to the words cast down there like thunder. There in his child's eyes, the fane exposed itself in ageless shadows, a place of still air and dark grey robes, the better to show the light, his father always said. The fane was a window to the gods' light, his father said, and the words cast a spell in Conry's mind. A doorway, his father said, into the unseen world that was the space of worship and of fear. For the fear of the gods is the love of the gods, as a child's fear of its father marks the strength of a father's love.

That spring, before she had set out for Brin and the master healers, Lady Jeslyn had begun to spend more time at the fane beyond the rites of the gods' day. At her private sacraments, Conry had watched as his father called down the strength of Crecinu the healer, and Lady Jeslyn had knelt bent at the altar and shuddered as the glow of animys suffused through her at his father's touch. And even so, Conry saw the weakness still in her as she climbed to her gig with its fine palfrey and set out through the haze of dust along the farm track for the manor and home.

That spring, Lady Jeslyn was dying. Her cousin-servants had spread that truth and rumor slowly, voice to ear to voice in the quiet of the market's morning, or the heat of afternoon when there was no strength for anything but quiet words. They told of what the future held and extracted promises of silence on pain of death, they said. On the threat of all the gods' wrath if Lady Jeslyn ever found out that the terrible truth had passed their lips.

In time, Lady Jeslyn was too weak even to drive the gig, yet still too proud to be driven. And so for one copper halak of his very own, Conry would walk the palfrey carefully along the track from the fane to the manor house, in the weeks before she had departed for Brin, seeking the healers who would tell her they could no longer help her frail body cling to life.

And as Conry walked, Lady Jeslyn spoke to him in a frail voice whose pain he heard, and she told him then, "You work hard, boy. You try your best, and you have the strength your father gives you."

And Conry answered, "Yes, my lady."

"You know your father's words," Lady Jeslyn said. "You know your father's strength better than almost any other. From where you sit and watch on the gods' day, I see you rapt, your eyes in close attention."

"Yes, my lady."

"Children are not made to understand," she said. "You do well to listen, though you are too young by far to know all you hear. For there are meanings. There are lessons yet unlearned, but you have the blazing light of wonder in your eyes, and this will lead you one day into the world of men, like your father. There is a lifetime to be spent in the wilderness of ignorance before the single day of understanding that comes unbidden at the gods' hands."

"Yes, my lady," Conry said, and he smiled back at her, at her sharp words of encouragement.

"You will learn the world as mysteries, as your father learned them, and when the gods' time is right, you will be made to know as all men are made to know who are touched. I see it in you. The light of knowledge and the mark of the gods that touches your brow. You listen to my words, boy. I know of more things than you know.

"Yes, my lady."

In the fane, Conry stood in his space of silence and listened as his father's words unfolded. On the gods' day, families filled the fane. All the children of the village were there, with whom the laughter of friendship passed on all other days. But on the gods' day, their eyes were cast over, faces dim with fear while his father spoke and hurled the words of the gods down like firebrands. All the folk of the village knelt rapt then. Somewhere at the centre of their hearts, the words burned and their souls trembled as Conry watched, looking past the silent strength in their limbs, farm folk tall and wind-burnt, faces that spoke of the solid strength of their lives, building on itself year after year.

Lady Jeslyn was different from the rest. Conry had always seen it. Lady Jeslyn alone showed no fear.

This morning of Lady Jeslyn's rites, no children knelt in the fane. Only the adults knelt in tight circles, straight-backed and still despite the heat, and there was a certain emptiness that looked back at him from the haze of eyes. Few children as a matter of course attended the rites of death and passing, with exceptions made for family. Infants in mothers' arms, turned quiet by the spirit of mourning, though far too young to understand. Young girls grown up in the space of the words that a eulogy makes. Young boys dressed in the black cloaks of the men they would one day become, eyes fixed on some point far away from the moment.

At his father's side, Conry had seen the rites of death and passing countless times, but always at a distance. Conry had his duty at the fane, to polish the altar stone, to empty the brazier, to sweep the worn flagstones clean before the high doors were opened to those who would assemble. At dawn that day, the bier had been carried in and he was already there, pushing his broom in the slow arcs that kept the dust down. With stony smooth faces that seemed to belie the heat already rising, the guards of the manor had carried Lady Jeslyn like an honor guard, and Conry saw her face dew fresh from the touch of his father's hand. The magic of animys replacing the glow that fades away when the spirit leaves the flesh.

In the heat and shadow of the rites, Conry saw his father touch Lady Jeslyn's cheek now. Just for a moment, brushing it lightly with a single finger. He stood tall and steel-grey in his priest's robe, looking down at the body beneath him like a smith might appraise a cooling blade, catching its light at angles to illuminate telltale blemishes, marks of weakness. He nodded to himself, and as he turned away, Conry saw the light ripple at the high window, cords of silver bound to the black oak of the bier gleaming as his father passed.

The morning of the day that Old Rhen died, the druid had twisted his staff of black oak in his hands as he sat in the green shadow of the riverbank. "I choose my deeds according to the custom of my mind," he said to Conry, "and my mind denies your gods. Yet some call my deeds memorable in their own right."

He stood with an ease that belied his age, and Conry stumbled back as a cloud of pale cottonwood tufts suddenly lifted from the ground to swirl around him. The druid tapped his fingers along the staff, and the cloud transformed to a swarm of snow-white butterflies that shimmered and danced and flitted away to the shadows.

Conry's eyes narrowed, suspicious, but Old Rhen laughed. "I can match your father and your grandfather's power in healing, but Crecinu has never heard my praise. I call down the clouds whose rain draws forth crops from the dust that was this land's only legacy before my kind came, but Denas is not my storm lord. So when you and your faithful call the rains, tell me why your gods are silent?"

"In the silence, we listen for the voices of the gods." The words were those of Conry's father once more, and he tried to feel for their strength even as he felt it suddenly flagging. "Silence is the fane's domain. Silence that cleanses the mind and focuses the heart that humbles itself before the gods. We pray in silence so that the gods echo our thoughts and our trembling when they speak."

Old Rhen laughed then, and Conry felt himself falling into the druid's eyes, bright like sunlight on clear water, their light swirling like the depths of a pleasant blindness. "And when do the gods speak? Have you heard them yourself, boy?"

"The gods speak through the voices of those who serve," Conry said, defiant. "Folk heard my grandfather at the altar when the fane was new built in the name of the gods returned. They heard the spell his voice cast and saw the fire in his eyes that burned all sin right out of them. That same fire burned in my father from the day he was born. The hand of the gods shaped him, and through him is the faith of folk shaped. It passed from his father to him, and it will pass to me as sure as the gods' word is the law of Gracia now and forevermore."

Old Rhen laughed again, and he spoke words that Conry did not understand. He felt the same faint shiver that he sensed in the presence of his father's magic, the healing touch that he had seen mend broken bone, broken minds, flesh ravaged by the darkest rot. Old Rhen raised his arms and a peal of thunder sounded out suddenly, and the sky was shrouded with a haze of cloud that had boiled in from nowhere.

A patter of rain started on the leaves overhead. A gentle sound, and the scent of clear water and the rising dust that it washed away.

"Believe in what you see, boy," Old Rhen said. "Believe in the world around you, and fear any god that speaks only through another's voice." But there was a peacefulness to his own voice. A contrast to the stern power in the words that were his father's, spoken in the shadow of the fane where they became the voices of the gods themselves.

Conry turned and ran, his tunic soaked and the scent of dust washed clear of him by the time he reached the fane.

"The words of the Orosana are the last words. And they have called Lady Jeslyn, and there is no response save acceptance and humility at our place in the gods and the fate they decree for us."

Tall at the altar, Conry's father bowed his head so that his hair hung to frame the shadow of his face. Quiet and tall and hard to the touch like a priest of the Orosana must be, his was the voice of the gods that rang out now with all the authority of life and death, stilling the hushed voices that had filled the fane. Closest to the altar and the bier, only Lady Jeslyn's servant-cousins still whispered, making benedictions that only they could hear.

"We are but shadows given form and life by the breath of the gods. Born in the darkness to which our doom returns us, we mark out our time beneath the gods' light of life. Our passage from shadow to shadow."

Where Conry stood at the altar door, his father appraised him with a backward glance, taking him in with the unblinking eyes that swallowed up the dim light like the grey of the robe that hung from his full shoulders. Conry stared back, tried not to blink but failed against the dust in his eyes, heavy on the air. He wiped a hand across his face.

Then his father turned away and Conry was gone. Into the shadows, through the door, and away to the bright light of morning beyond. He took one last look at Lady Jeslyn as he went.

"She knew the gods," his father tolled. "She kept their names holier than any other, looking always to the light." And as Conry broke into a run, all he could think on was that the veil of death shrouds faith as well as life. Lady Jeslyn was dead. Shrunken there on her bier, she could have been anyone. No way to tell what she believed anymore.

Conry raced along the grass, the narrow stretch of brittle green along the edge of the road, shored off by stands of dust-streaked witchwillow that clawed the clear blue sky. The wind was warmer where it pushed out of the stirring woods once more, the sun above the trees now and climbing quickly, and there would be light within the fane soon enough.

As Conry sprinted past, dust devils sparred between silent wains and carriages, trying in vain to erase the record of tracks that mark off the number of people this day has brought. Conry buried his face in his sleeve but swallowed the scent of dust all the same. In the fane or on the wind, no difference. Within, grey light. Without, the gritty air and the tall trees, the stir of green that marked the passage of the faint breeze.

The fane stood on the hillside, the scrubland falling away below, down to the river bottom where the breeze was born. On the other side, the village, houses bunched in small patches of color along dust-streaked road. The small farm cottages were beyond that, but already waves of heat hid them. If Conry squinted, he could make them out, just barely. He tried to listen for sounds coming up off the hazed image below, hearing only the silence rise. The quiet of an empty memory, the people snatched out and brought here, set down in the stifling fane to whisper Lady Jeslyn's name this one last time.

The village looked as ever it did, as if Conry might have already stood, might yet stand on this hill his whole life watching, seeing nothing change. Standing alone against time, everything within this single pane of vision cut from eternal cloth. Everything the same, the village, the fane always standing, never fading away.

People change, he thought. People die. Lady Jeslyn. Old Rhen.

Life was the first gift of the gods, his father said, and death the doorway through which the gods call all folk home. Death was the gods' final gift, and the reckoning of all folk's lives to be made in the gods' names.

Conry believed it. All his life, he had believed it.

"Boy..."

He ran harder, the dead voice of Old Rhen calling him on.

The wind blew clear the night that Lady Jeslyn and Old Rhen died, and Conry had followed the river past dusk before pursuing his father to the fane. From the time his mother died, it had been the ritual of endless days for both. After the evening meal, his father knelt at the altar alone to work in the solitude and the silence, and when Conry was done with cleaning and his lessons at home, he would follow his father there.

All the scrolls, all the writings that were his father's work were kept in racks behind the altar, and Conry would reseal the parchments left open by his father from the previous day, carefully powdering and drying the stark ink of his new writings, page by page. As he did, he would read them. Hoping always to glean the wisdom there.

At night, the candles were cold above the silent flagstones. The altar stone was a smooth shadow, the glowing brazier behind it showing as a pool of red-black flame. Conry patiently watched his father work, listening to his murmured words as they rose to summon up the voice of wisdom that was promised him long ago, and which he still waited to understand.

The night that Lady Jeslyn and Old Rhen died, Conry had stopped along the way to the fane. Running as he always did, he stared out to the burning copper sky to see a figure making its way quickly along the river trail. The distance was too great for faces, the shadows too deep. But he thought he knew that figure by its slender form, by the black gown she always wore, recognizing Lady Jeslyn by her walk. Remembering the spring, when he helped her down from the gig and held her frail weight on his arm as she paced slowly to the manor house. She circled as she moved, arms open as if she might have been searching for something, beckoning, face turned to the sky. But then she saw him and started, and as if she feared that sudden sight, she turned quickly, stumbling through the high arch of trees to vanish into the bright haze of setting sun beyond.

She moved more quickly than Conry expected, but still he feared for her, outside and alone. Worrying for her ability to find her way back to the manor house again, and so he followed her. And when he did, he saw in himself for a moment the figure of his father as he walked the farmhouse roads to folk in need of his healer's hands. He tried to compose himself in the manner of the straight shoulders and the long strides, and inside, he felt the hunger for understanding, for wisdom, that burned as strong as ever. That knowledge always kept waiting, marked by a patience for which he prayed to Denas, to Danassa, for the strength to maintain. Waiting for this childhood of his to end and for the understanding of men, for the power that was his father's, to come to him at long last.

Lady Jeslyn had disappeared within the shadow of the cottonwoods whose tufted fingers bade farewell to the blood-red sun. Conry broke from his measured stride, moving quickly to catch up to her, determined to catch sight of the one he would shepherd, the one he would protect as his father was the protector of so many.

He was running, worry turning in his mind, when he sprinted into the shadow of the great willow and stumbled upon what was left of Old Rhen.

He recognized the druid by his robe of unwashed homespun, and by the lines of black ink that twisted like dark lightning up his arms. But those robes were shredded and drenched with blood that turned black in the falling light, the broken arms up in a gesture that at first seemed a sign of some great and final fear. A covering of the eyes, of warding away the final sight of life.

But as Conry stepped closer, heart pounding, throat tight with a dryness more bitter than any dust, he saw the look of defiance trapped for this last endless moment in the tree-priest's wide-open eyes. He saw the fingers gnarled not in a gesture of warding, but in the spellsign that was alike in the magic of druid and animyst, of Old Rhen and his father alike.

Whatever had killed Old Rhen, the druid had fought it, defiant, even as it shattered his bones and turned his flesh ashen and left the flow of his life draining to the black earth.

Conry staggered as his stomach heaved, the taint of acid and dark bile flooding him as he fell to his knees.

"Boy…"

The voice was a night-dark whisper in his mind, and Conry choked off a cry as he fell back, scrambling away from the body. In the shadow, he saw the old druid yet unmoving, no sign of breath where the dark homespun was distended by shattered ribs.

"Boy…" the voice said again, and Conry felt it unfold a message that he understood as feeling and memory more than words. He shook his head, desperate, frantic, but the voice held on tight, set itself in his mind like a creature of claw and shadow. He felt his head turn as if held by unseen hands, felt himself lurch along the bank to a place that the voice wanted him to go, but he fought it.

Then he ran.

It was summer, and Conry had the summer strength in his legs, and then suddenly over his shoulder, the silver gleam of the just-risen Clearmoon to light his way across the scrub. He didn't remember the journey, mind blank until it caught sight of the fane rising before him in the moon's-light.

As Conry slipped into the looming archway of the trees now, the sunlight fractured and the green shadow deepened above the slow flow of water, an archway of branches widening before him in the dark. The path made its way between twisted trunks and root hollows, leading to the creek where it shadowed the trade road's winding course toward the village. Conry moved blindly down its familiar course until the morning's light faded further into shadow, and the only sound was the wind and there was no fane at all behind him, lost beyond the high hill if he had turned to look.

At the creek's edge, he slowed, fighting to breathe. He didn't know how long his father would speak, no idea how much time he might have. Above him somewhere, the sun still whispered warmth but the shadows around him spoke of twilight that never broke, the overhanging trees rippling in sullen waves along the water.

"Boy..."

Old Rhen's voice in his mind was a fading echo after five days, and Conry knew that if he left it alone, if he ignored it long enough, it would dim to silence as all echoes do. But he saw the stain of blood still visible across the loam that had been Old Rhen's only bier. Then he walked ten paces past it, toward the place the voice had directed him that night, and from which he had turned away.

"This is the old magic," the voice said. *"You pray to your gods for proof against fear, but the darkness holds fears whose faces prove the falseness of your gods. Life alone has the power to break that darkness, but its power must be guided by one unsullied by the dark's touch."*

"Where are you?" Conry whispered, and the voice only laughed.

He saw the dagger then. It was a mundane-looking blade, its handle carved of bone and the steel etched and pitted with long use. It lay a half-dozen strides from where the body had fallen, stuck into the ground as if thrust there, and the hand's-breadth of its blade showing above the earth had been etched with a mark that still glowed white with the telltale sign of spellcraft. A sigil of twisted lines whose shape echoed the lightning lines that had marked the old druid's arms.

"This is my life, boy. This is the old magic..."

By night or day, there was silence here beneath the trees, but it was different than the silence that the fane created. The fane an echo, somehow, its walls playing back the shadows of earlier movement even when all was empty. Recreating the voices that spoke in cold tones, men and women kneeling before the altar that was the reminder of the cold strength of those they served.

Conry pulled the dagger from the ground. Afraid to touch it that night, he had run instead, the dead druid's voice echoing in his head until his screams had drowned it out. But he felt the cool weight of the blade in his hand now. Above him, the twisting trees spread a blank veil of green, dropping down across the water, nearly touching it. He felt the space around him as a measure of black shadow, a gateway with no depth where the light faded and the creek disappeared and all that was left was the sound of water against banks of sand, slowly sculpted by time. The power of this place, of a dead man's life channeled to cold steel.

Lady Jeslyn was dead, and Old Rhen was dead, and everything had changed.

The door was unlocked when Conry had burst into the fane that night. Breathless, alert, he hung shaking on the brass handle of the door to see the nave bright with candlelight, shimmering gold that spilled out into the darkness. Firelight played across the walls as a show of shadow puppets. He staggered in, aware of his footsteps, his voice crying out his father's name in fear, shattering the sacred silence. He needed his father, needed to tell him what he had seen. Old Rhen was dead. His father would know what to do.

At the altar, darkness wove a pattern of twisting lines. It hung there even against the candlelight in a way that Conry didn't understand. His father was on his back in that darkness, stretched out across the altar stone, and standing there watching, Conry heard his father's voice cry out, strained as if heard across some great distance. Then his father spoke, indistinct, uttering over and over again the name of the creature that loomed above him, and Conry heard that creature, and it spoke no words but he knew its voice all the same. He knew the tone, the laughter turned dark as it drowned the voice of Old Rhen where it twisted through his mind.

The creature was mottled red and black, naked as a babe but full in the ripeness of womanhood. Its face was Lady Jeslyn's, but she was young, as Conry had never seen her. Hair the black of a raven's wing plunged down her back, twined between her surging breasts, twisted into the darker tangle between her thighs where she held herself astride his father and impaled herself on the shadowed pillar of his sex again and again. A shroud of wings enclosed her, unfurling to beat the air with each furious stroke of her dark body, wreathed in a flame that gave no smoke, no heat.

His father stared with wide eyes from beneath her, slack-jawed and rapt, and crying out in a voice wracked with a sadness and a hunger Conry had never known outside the space of empty memory where his mother's touch was held.

He stumbled back, and in the darkness, fell. The floor where he sprawled was dust, a thick patina that bled from aging stone, choking off his air as he tried to cough but could not, no room in his lungs for breath.

With a shriek, the creature tore herself free of his father and crossed the fane in a single pulse of black wings. The anger of the gods was in her eyes, Conry saw, a faint flicker of black that spread to blue flame, almost too faint to see. Her smile was wide, lips the red of blood, the red of her tongue where she tasted the air, tasted his fear as he scrambled back. Her face was stone, etched with fury and lines of leering contempt that touched the corners of her mouth. Blood welled up in Conry's eyes, at his groin, the creature that was Lady Jeslyn sliding lithely toward him on slick limbs, her sculpted breasts pendulous and swaying, clasped wet to him suddenly as he slammed his back against the door, nowhere to go as she pressed close.

He felt the rage in her, a thing so sharp that it would cut if he let it touch him. Her hair twisted as if driven by a storm wind, wrapping Conry like black snakes, and she ran her fingers along his heaving chest, across his dry lips, down his belly to twist the ache below into an even greater torment.

"You dare..."

It was Lady Jeslyn's voice, a whisper in ears and mind at once, echoing in Conry's bones and blood. She rose before him into the light, grasping him one-handed at the throat and lifting him as if he weighed nothing, and Conry was battered by the power in her black eyes, his mouth seared, tongue thick, his breath turned to dust as he shook his head frantically, no.

No, my lady. He mouthed the words. *Forgive me,* but no sound escaped the parched pain of his throat, then that dryness was countered by a sudden spurting wetness across his belly, and he could no longer stand, convulsing as he sunk to the floor.

With Old Rhen's dagger in hand, Conry raced back through the light. The straight line across the treed scrubland, skirting the farm track and the dust that rose there with the passing of a goat herd, bleating cries fading as he raced past. Running fast on summer-strong legs, he felt the heat of the sun, molten gold at his back now.

By the time he returned to the fane, it was over. The folk of village and farm shuffled out slowly, tired faces in small groups, voices low against the hiss of hot wind and the restless voices of the horses as the wains left the field one by one. Grey haze trailed out along the road as they passed, making their way to the village to wait out the time until they would gather again at the manor house where Lady Jeslyn's pyre would burn. They would watch her given up to the dust, scattered on the high hillside as she would have wanted, overlooking the forest where her husband had perished all those years ago.

Dark eyes met Conry's without seeing as he made his way in at the altar door. One by one, the last folk in the fane turned away, faces drawn, hands held tightly to their sides. An air of finality, of resignation, hung like a smoke that lingers long after the burning is done. The airborne memory of some elemental fear. The heat was heavy even to compare to the sun outside, the bitter wind.

Three men robed in black like all the rest stood at the bier and bent close, some whispered word passing between them. Then they turned away and Conry saw the shadow flicker in their wake as they joined the withering crowd. And where it touched Lady Jeslyn's pale face, grey shadow created the illusion of movement there. A ripple like the catching of a last shuddering breath.

Conry blinked. Lady Jeslyn lay unmoving, sealed behind faint bars of sunbeam slanting down through the high windows at last, playing in the ornate scrollwork along the bier's edge.

At the altar, blood-red in the light of the brazier, a parchment sheet lay folded. It had the look of his father's work but was clean and unblemished, unmarked by the hard-edged script that fell from his father's hands. Conry picked it up by absent reflex, but as he turned to the scroll racks behind him, he heard a faint ringing as something struck the ground.

He knelt, shadow filling his sight as he saw where a black gemstone had slipped out of the parchment. It bore the same sigil of twisted lines that had marked the blade of the dagger at the river's edge, slipping out where it was tucked within the whiteness of the sheet. Conry unfolded the parchment to see where it had blackened to the stone's touch.

That dark night in the fane, the creature that was Lady Jeslyn kissed him, and Conry had felt a sudden stirring as the power of her dark faith coursed through him. He felt the strength in her, felt the empty echo of his father's gasping cry in the darkness beyond his sight, and the knowledge of the gods that had been passed from grandfather to father and was waiting now for him. All the words to wait for, the words of the gods that only men know, that he would know as his father and

Lady Jeslyn knew. The world outside his own child's mind that he was heir to. Their world of faith.

"You understand, boy?" she said, and he felt the sweet burning of her breath against his neck.

"Yes, my lady," Conry whispered.

"The gods' time is right, and you will be made to know as all men are made to know."

"Yes, my lady…"

"Life has the power to break the darkness. Believe in what you see, boy…"

Old Rhen's voice in his head sent a shiver through him that was a shimmer of rain-soaked breeze. Through the tears that wracked him as Lady Jeslyn laughingly lifted him closer, Conry saw a glint of black shadow. Set between her breasts, ridged with dark lines where her skin clutched at it, a black gemstone gleamed.

Without thinking, Conry shot his hand up, feeling a sudden numbness slam through his arm like the kick of a horse as he grabbed the gem. His fingers were deadened but he felt them sink in just the same, digging into flesh that was soft like clay, cold as ice, burning like fire.

He heard Lady Jeslyn's voice ring out as a shriek of pain, and she was striking at him, raking his arm with taloned fingers.

Then she was sprawled on the ground at Conry's feet and the black gem was pulsing in his hand, and it was Lady Jeslyn again, her naked body stooped and bent, withered and gnarled with the age of ninety-six summers and the consumption that had sent her to the master healers at the temples in Brin. Her open eyes were lifeless within the shadow of her grey-white hair. Her mouth was wide, no breath tracing the withered dugs that sprawled against her chest.

No one will ever know where Lady Jeslyn went once the master healers turned her away.

Conry felt the black gem slip from his grasp as his father cried out, unseen at the altar. He didn't look back as he ran.

The manor guards were the only ones left in the fane, the press of mourners thinned to nothing now. Conry's father was gone, stepping out into the pale morning and the hushed voices of those who remained. The guards approached the dais, the stooped figure in the lead carrying the shroud that would cover Lady Jeslyn as they carried the litter back to the manor.

Conry's voice caught them as they approached the altar.

"My father calls for you outside."

They turned as one, seeing the young master at the main doors and the priest his father standing with his back to them in the haze of light beyond. They hadn't seen him slip past them through the shadows, hadn't seen him close and lock the smaller doors at altar and brazier before he did.

They dutifully nodded, marching back into the light and through, and Conry had the main doors closed and barred in a half-dozen hammerings of his frantic heart.

He ran to the altar, fighting the fear that was a stone in his gut. He felt the grey light as much as saw it, felt the dust at his eyes and in the quickness of his breath.

His hand was shaking as he pulled the black gem from his pocket, but he had stilled it by the time he touched it down to the flesh of Lady Jeslyn's neck.

A pulse of sanguine light flared, and its gleam was blood at his hands and along the floor and all the walls suddenly, and Lady Jeslyn's pale skin shivered with the sudden touch of breath and life as her eyes flicked open wide.

Conry heard the sudden pounding at the door behind him, his father or the manor guard or both realizing that he had sealed himself in. He heard the rising laughter of the creature that was Lady Jeslyn as she smiled wide, the force of her life inside his head suddenly, inside his heart and scouring his shivering skin like a dark caress.

He had Old Rhen's dagger already in hand, plunging down to shatter ribs and pierce Lady Jeslyn's dead heart.

The creature cried out once. The red-black haze of light fractured like the frailest ceramic, shedding itself as it faded and was broken by a pulse of blue-white that shattered the gem and cracked the blade with a sound like thunder.

Another crack, the bar breaking at the door behind him.

The body on the bier was dust, a haze of blackened grit sifting to the air and floor. It swirled as if attempting to hold onto its shape, faint tendrils snatching at each other, and then it was gone.

Conry heard the footsteps behind him falter, a choking off of voices, an anger held in sudden check. A whispered benediction was recognized as his father's voice. He heard a sigh and distant laughter that he recognized as Old Rhen, fading finally from his mind.

"No, my lady," the druid's voice said.

Outside, Conry heard the faint hiss of rain kiss the parched ground.

Conry turned to his father, not meeting his gaze where he and the manor guards faltered before the altar, staring at the haze of grey that unfurled from the form of the body that had lain there and now was gone. A haze of grey hung in the sky through the open doors, cloud that had boiled in from nowhere.

He rubbed his eyes of dust and let the scent of rain slip through him. He felt the light wax and wane as he walked from stifling heat to open air, pushing past his father, stepping from shadow to shadow.

"No, my lady…"

Fiction by
Scott Fitzgerald Gray

WE CAN BE HEROES

A PRAYER FOR DEAD KINGS and Other Tales

CLEARWATER DAWN — Book One of "The Exile's Blade"

BLACKHEATH (with Quinn Hamilton)

THE VOICES OF THE DEAD — Dark Tales & Lost Souls

TALES OF THE ENDLANDS
The Twilight Child • Shadow to Shadow • The Moonsign Scar
Daeralf's Rune • The Game of Heart and Light • The Voice
Black Run •A Space Between • Stories

ONE SIZE FITS ALL (as Gary Scott)

Scott Fitzgerald Gray is a specially constructed biogenetic simulacrum built around an array of experimental consciousness-sharing techniques — a product of the finest minds of Canadian science until the grant money ran out. Accidentally set loose during an unauthorized midnight rave at the lab, the S.F. Gray entity is currently at large amongst an unsuspecting populace, where his work as an author, screenwriter, editor, RPG designer, and story editor for feature film keeps him off the streets.

More info on Scott and his work (some of it even occasionally truthful) can be found by reading between the lines at **insaneangel.com**.

Colophon

From over the length of time that these tales have been in the making, the following are profusely thanked for inspiration, patience, feedback, and just generally kicking creative ass.

Manor and Home
Colleen, Shvaugn, and Caitlin

The Intelligence Branch
Colleen Craig, Gabriel Duclair, Mitchell Wylie

On Exhibition in the White Tower Gallery
(studio)Effigy, Prill, DarkOne, Kojoku, Jose A.S. Reyes, Jeff Thrower

Keepers of the Old Stories
Tori Amos, François Bertrand, Blue October, Storn Cook,
Daft Punk, Dead Can Dance, John Debney, Ramin Djawadi,
Darrin Drader, Harlan Ellison, William Faulkner, Lisa Gerrard,
Murray Gold, Jennifer Landels, Colin McComb, Edgar Allan Poe,
Kristine Kathryn Rusch, Rush, Jeremy Soule, Gary Wright

The VOICES of the DEAD

Dark Tales & Lost Souls
An Anthology of the Endlands

by
Scott Fitzgerald Gray

Published by Insane Angel Studios
insaneangel.com

Cover Design and Typography by (studio)Effigy
From an image by Prill

ISBN 978-1-927348-25-3

v1.0
December 2012

*We try to make sure that no errors creep into our work, but publishing is a chaotic
enterprise at the best of times. If you spot a typo or a formatting glitch in an Insane Angel
Studios book, email insaneangel@insaneangel.com with details (including which e-book
version you're reading, if applicable). If any errors you spot are ones we haven't yet caught
and are in the process of fixing, you'll receive one of our e-books of your choice for free.*

www.ingramcontent.com/pod-product-compliance
Lightning Source LLC
Chambersburg PA
CBHW071320130626
46556CB00004B/1671